KATE WALKER

The Unexpected Child

Harlequin Books

TORONTO • NEW YORK • LONDON
AMSTERDAM • PARIS • SYDNEY • HAMBURG
STOCKHOLM • ATHENS • TOKYO • MILAN
MADRID • WARSAW • BUDAPEST • AUCKLAND

ISBN 0-373-11921-6

THE UNEXPECTED CHILD

First North American Publication 1997.

Copyright © 1997 by Kate Walker.

This edition published by arrangement with Harlequin Books S.A.

® and TM are trademarks of the publisher. Trademarks indicated with
® are registered in the United States Patent and Trademark Office, the
Canadian Trade Marks Office and in other countries.

Printed in U.S.A.

KATE WALKER

The Unexpected Child

Harlequin Books

TORONTO • NEW YORK • LONDON
AMSTERDAM • PARIS • SYDNEY • HAMBURG
STOCKHOLM • ATHENS • TOKYO • MILAN
MADRID • WARSAW • BUDAPEST • AUCKLAND

ISBN 0-373-11921-6

THE UNEXPECTED CHILD

First North American Publication 1997.

by Kate Walker

UIN PRESENTS
TING WITH DANGER

any of our special offers. Write to us at the
ddress for information on our newest releases.

Reader Service
Walden Ave., P.O. Box 1325, Buffalo, NY 14269
P.O. Box 609, Fort Erie, Ont. L2A 5X3

CHAPTER ONE

As NATALIE let herself out of the house, the clock in the dining room struck the half-hour, making her stop dead at the sudden realisation that just twelve hours had passed since she had opened the same door on the previous night. Barely half a day, and yet the impact of that time on her life was immeasurable; it would never be the same again.

If she had stuck to her original impulse to ignore the summons of the doorbell, then this would have been just a normal Monday morning, her thoughts only of the coming weeks, with their lead up to Christmas and its pantomime, nativity play and all the other activities the school would be involved in. But the bell had rung again, more insistently, it seemed, and, realising belatedly that with the lights on and the curtain wide open she could hardly pretend not to be at home, she'd got to her feet reluctantly.

'What is it?'

Impatience rang in her tone as she pulled the door open, letting in a blast of cold night air that made her shiver in spite of the warmth of the cherry-red tunic-length sweater she wore with black stretch leggings. An icy wind blew a couple of strands of her dark hair into her heart-shaped face.

'Just what—?'

The words died on her tongue, her brown eyes opening wide, as the light from the hallway spilled out onto the tall, masculine figure standing at the top of the steps.

'Hi, Nat.'

In spite of the painful familiarity of the voice, Natalie had to blink hard in order to convince herself that she really was seeing clearly.

'Pierce?'

It was all she could manage, shock numbing her brain so that she found it impossible to think. More than ten years ago, she had been knocked completely off balance the first time she had ever seen Pierce Donellan, and since then she had never been able to recover any degree of mental equilibrium where he was concerned.

He still had the power to deprive her of speech, the impact of his forcefully male attraction positively lethal to any hope of composure. Even casually dressed as he was now, in worn jeans and a navy sweatshirt, under a black leather jacket, with his black hair blown wildly around his head by the wind, and raindrops scattered like diamonds amongst the jet strands, he had a heart-stopping male beauty that closed her throat and drove coherent thought from her mind.

'Nothing to say, Nat?' That cool voice was threaded through with a note of mockery that she remembered with a sense of discomfort from the past. 'That isn't like you. You always seemed to have plenty of opinions, and were only too keen to make sure that I heard every one of them.'

'You took me by surprise—you were the last person I expected to see.'

And that was the absolute truth. She had long since convinced herself that Pierce Donellan would never again be part of her life, and if some weak, impressionable piece of her heart had still retained the foolish hope that things could be otherwise, then the news that had set the whole village buzzing only the previous month would have put paid to that.

'To what do I owe the honour of this visit?'

Pierce's grin in response to her unsettled tartness was disturbingly boyish, even slightly shamefaced, the appeal of that lopsided smile winging its way to her frighteningly vulnerable heart and tugging at it sharply. After believing that she had lost him for ever, she couldn't suppress the rush of joy that flooded through her to see him like this, and yet stern realism told her that she would only be laying herself open to more hurt if she let him just wander back into her life as he had always done before.

'Would you believe I was just passing?'

'No way.'

Still not sure how to take him, she tried to harden her heart against him, knowing with a sense of despair that it was a vain attempt. One more smile like that one and she was done for.

'Not even you could be "just passing" Holme Road on the way to anywhere. For one thing, it's a cul-de-sac, and for an—'

'OK, I confess! I was on my way to hide out at the Manor when I realised that with my mother away at Angela's there would be no one around. The housekeeper's on holiday so the place will be deserted, the heating off, so I thought it would be the perfect opportunity to look up an old friend.'

'"Old friend?"' Natalie echoed, injecting a note of scepticism into her words and struggling to make herself feel something of the same emotion—an effort that was weakened as Pierce moved more into the light so that she saw with some concern how pale and drawn he looked. Or perhaps that was just the effect of the moonlight draining all the colour from his skin.

'Don't you think that's something of an exaggeration? The truth is simply that my mother was your family's cook and housekeeper for some years and you occasionally condescended to speak to me.'

Oh, why couldn't time have given her some degree of objectivity? Why couldn't absence have put a distance between her and this man so that, if not exactly out of sight, out of mind, then at least she might have had a chance of facing him with some sort of confidence?

With anyone else, she could behave as the mature professional of twenty-four she was. But Pierce seemed to be able to strip away the intervening years with a glance, reducing her once more to the gauche and rather prickly adolescent she had been when they had first met, a situation that was made all the worse by the knowledge that her foolish dreams had been just that—fantasies, without a hope of coming true.

'And you were never exactly a regular visitor even when you lived in Ellerby. That would be too much like slumming for the Lord of the Manor. I can't imagine what brings you here—'

'You know I always hated that nickname!' Pierce's words cut in on her, cold and hard as his expression. 'If I'm not welcome, you only have to say.'

Already he was turning away. He was perfectly capable of leaving without another word, Natalie realised—prepared to walk out of her life as easily as he had strolled back into it, and with no further explanation. Stern common sense said she should let him go, but her heart cried out in protest at the thought. It was almost three years since she had last seen him. If he went now, would she ever see him again?

'Well, now you're here, the least I can do is offer you a cup of coffee!' she said, pushing aside her hesitation as she opened the door wider. 'Come in before you freeze, and...'

Her voice faded as she turned from closing the door to find him standing so close behind her that her arm brushed against his as she moved. In the dark confines of the hallway, he seemed somehow bigger, much more forceful than ever before, making her feel even less than her average five feet five. The lean, strong frame seemed to fill the small space so completely that she was suddenly gripped by the unnerving feeling of being trapped alongside some powerful jungle cat, with no idea when or even if it planned to pounce on its potential prey.

'Go into the living room,' she said hastily, knowing she sounded as disturbed as she felt. She could think of no possible reason why Pierce should seek her out like this after all this time. 'There's a fire in there; it'll soon warm you up.'

The unexpected tension that had tugged at her nerves also drove her to switch on the main overhead light as she followed him into the room, not feeling at ease with the shadows cast by her small desk lamp. Her first sight of Pierce in the sudden brightness had her taking a step back in surprise.

'Are you all right?'

He looked dreadful, she acknowledged privately, his skin drawn tight over the strong bones of his face in a way that etched lines around his mouth and eyes, and the pallor she had noted earlier and now saw was not just a trick of the moonlight made him look drained and haggard, an effect that was aggravated by the dark stubble that shadowed his cheeks.

'Just tired.'

Pierce rubbed the back of his hand over his eyes, but not before she had glimpsed, and worried over, the unnatural, almost feverish glitter that burned in their sapphire depths.

'The motorway was hellish—the world and his wife seemed to be on their way to somewhere from somewhere tonight.'

'Everyone would be trying to get home at the last minute after the holiday, I suppose.' Taking her cue from his casual dismissal of her concern, Natalie tried to make her words sound light and more relaxed than she actually felt. 'They'd want to be back in time for school tomorrow.'

'Yeah, that'd be it—I'd forgotten it was half-term.'

The blue eyes went to the desk in the corner, the clutter of papers highlighted by the glow of the lamp, and he frowned swiftly.

'Oh, hell—I'm sorry—you were working and I've interrupted you.'

'Not at all! I'd just finished.'

Mentally Natalie crossed her fingers against the white lie. Every instinct she possessed told her something was wrong—because she didn't believe that 'old friends' routine for one moment.

'So—can I get you something to drink? Coffee?'

'I'd rather have something stronger if you've got it.'

'There's only sherry.'

'Sherry will be fine.'

It was as she handed him the drink that another thought occurred to her, making her wonder if in fact alcohol was the best thing for him.

'Have you eaten?' It was the question she should have asked before she had poured him the sherry, she told herself reprovingly.

'Not since lunch. I didn't want to waste time by stopping for food—I wanted to get away from London as quickly as possible.'

'Was it as bad as that?'

'You'd better believe it.' Pierce took a swallow of his drink and she was glad to see that a trace of colour returned to his cheeks. 'I broke the speed limit almost all the way here.'

Which seemed to imply much more than just a casual visit home—and Pierce's beloved Porsche was capable of some very high speeds indeed. That thought had Natalie moving hastily to the window, twitching aside the curtain and looking down into the street, concerned for the safety of the expensive vehicle. This area of town suffered particularly from the problem of joyriders. As he watched her, Pierce's mouth twisted sharply.

'You needn't worry.' The dark irony of his tone stung bitterly. 'I parked the car a couple of streets away. No one will know that I'm here.'

'That wasn't what was bothering me.'

'Oh, wasn't it?'

His voice was harsher now, dangerously reminiscent of the anger that had been in it on the night of her eighteenth birthday, the night that had finally destroyed any chance that she and Pierce could ever regard each other as anything remotely resembling friends.

'According to you, you're the one with the reputation to lose.'

If his earlier comment had distressed her, this one actually had her mouth opening on a shocked gasp, a rush of anger driving away any pain it might have brought.

'And what about you?' Natalie retorted. 'Don't you think it might damage *your* reputation to be seen calling on—?'

'On one of the lowly peasants on the family estate?'

The coldly drawled question had Natalie taking an instinctive step or two backwards away from him. She had only ever seen Pierce in this sort of mood once before and it had frightened her then as it did now.

'On the contrary, my dear Natalie, I would have thought that it would very much enhance my reputation if people knew I was here.'

His intonation had changed again. This time the words were smokily sensuous, seeming to coil round her thoughts, clouding them, mesmerising her.

'What about the *droit du seigneur* that I'm supposed to lay claim to—the one thing I want from innocents like you?'

Inwardly, Natalie winced in response to his deliberate reminder of the words she had flung at him long ago, in a haze of hurt and anger. Then, as now, he had smiled as he spoke, but without any real warmth, his mood seeming light-years away from anything even vaguely resembling amusement, except of the darkest, harshest kind.

'After all, Ellerby is positively medieval in so many of its attitudes—don't you think that as Lord of the Manor I should be able to take my pick of the local village maidens?'

'Pierce—' Natalie tried huskily but he ignored her and, with that smile that made her think fearfully of a lazy tiger indolently surveying its prey, moved smoothly and silently to her side, lifting one hand to brush the backs of his fingers slowly down her cheek, making her shiver in involuntary response.

'If I can find any—maidens, that is,' he went on as if she hadn't spoken. 'They're something of a rarity these days. Most modern girls are so knowing—sure of themselves—so—'

He broke off abruptly, staring down into her heart-shaped face with an intensity that had her drawing in a quick, sharp breath and holding on to it, afraid to let it go.

'But not you, Nat—with those big doe's eyes and that innocent face...' A soft thumb brushed the fullness of her mouth. 'You're so very different.'

Suddenly he frowned, making her heart lurch in apprehension. In spite of the fact that he wasn't even touching her now, she felt trapped, held transfixed, like a rabbit petrified by the headlights of an oncoming car.

And like that terrified rabbit she knew instinctively that her situation was filled with danger, that by staying still she was risking pain and destruction for herself. She had to do something to stop this.

But even as her mind recognised that fact and screamed frantic instructions to her limbs to run to safety it was as if the fear itself had paralysed her and she couldn't move an inch.

'But I don't like the way you've started to do your hair,' Pierce murmured, gesturing towards the neat coil with undisguised scorn. 'It's too *tight*—too controlled. You look like a schoolmistress.'

'I *am* a schoolmistress.'

'Not now—not at this time of night. Now you're off duty, and so—'

Before she could realise what he had in mind, he had moved swiftly, his hands going unerringly to the pins that held the long, dark swathe of her hair confined at the back of her head. With two confident tugs he freed them, smiling with disturbingly sensual satisfaction as the ebony mane tumbled round her neck in waving disarray.

'Much better,' he declared, and then, to her complete consternation, he combed his fingers gently through the tumbled strands, smoothing them onto her shoulders with a touch so soft and gentle that it was all she could do not to close her eyes in languorous response, her lips parting to shape a murmur of delight that she only just choked back in time, realising it had been in the form of his name.

'Now you look positively kissable—in fact—'

'No!' Natalie cut in swiftly, suddenly afraid to hear more. The bitter irony of the situation struck home like a poisoned knife with the thought that years ago, even just a month or two before, she would actually have welcomed the sort of things he was saying—or, at least, the things she thought he was saying. Because the way he spoke was so darkly sardonic, those brilliant blue eyes holding no degree of warmth, that she couldn't be absolutely sure. But now, even if he did mean them, it was far too late. He was committed to another woman, and all his compliments should go to her.

'*Pierce.*' She tried hard to make it sound firmly determined but didn't succeed very well. 'You can't say things like that when you don't mean them.'

'And how do you know what I mean and what I don't? Have you suddenly become telepathic, so that you can see into my mind?'

The faint downward movement of his dark head was positively the last straw, bringing with it a bitter memory of the one and only time he had ever kissed her. The image sliced into the trance that held her still, shattering it with the realisation of the way she was tempting fate by not resisting.

'And what would your *fiancée* think about that?'

She made her voice as cool and crisp as she could but was a prey to distinctly ambiguous feelings as she saw the effect her words had, freezing that downward movement instantly, Pierce's eyes becoming suddenly hooded and withdrawn.

'I understand that congratulations are in order.'

From the way his face changed she knew that she had had the effect that she wanted—or, rather, the result that she had aimed for. What she had *wanted* was very, very different, and only now, with the possibility—or did she mean the *threat*?—that he might kiss her clearly averted, did she realise just how much she had wanted that caress, wanted it so desperately that the ache of loss that tormented her now made her clench her fingers into tight fists, nails digging into the palms of her hands.

'I'd forgotten how quickly the village gossip grapevine works.'

'So it's true.'

'Yeah, it's true.' Pierce's voice was strangely flat. 'I proposed to Phillippa a couple of months ago and she said yes straight away.'

I'll bet she did, Natalie thought, the taste of jealousy like bitter acid in her mouth. No woman with red blood in her veins would turn down Pierce Donellan, even if he didn't come with the added attraction of a private fortune—one that he had personally doubled over the last ten years or so as a result of the brilliant business acumen that had made his computer software company a major force to be reckoned with.

'So what are you doing here? Why aren't you with her?'

Why had he strolled back into her life, destroying the sort of acceptance she had achieved?

'A little tricky,' Pierce murmured sardonically, 'seeing as she's off on holiday—a Mediterranean cruise.'

'A cruise?'

It seemed a strange thing for a newly engaged woman to do. If Pierce had asked *her* to marry him, there was no way she would have left his side unless she absolutely had to.

'It was all arranged before we got engaged. She'd promised to go with her cousin.'

Something about his voice, the total lack of expression in his face heightened Natalie's conviction that something was wrong, that he hadn't just come here on the off chance as he'd said.

'Pierce—why *have* you come here tonight?'

Broad shoulders under the supple leather lifted in an indifferent shrug.

'To see a friendly face—totalk.'

'About what?'

The change in his eyes worried her.

'Tell me,' she insisted. '*What* did you want to talk about?'

For a long, taut moment he considered the question, the blue gaze strangely dull and unfocused. Then at last he seemed to come to a decision.

'About Phillippa,' he said, his voice harsh and raw. 'About my fiancée—or, rather, *ex*-fiancée, seeing as she's dumped me.'

CHAPTER TWO

'SHE'S—?'

Natalie couldn't believe what she was hearing. She had to have it all wrong—he must have said something else.

'Phillippa—she—? But I don't understand.'

'My fiancée has dumped me—broken off our engagement. To put it bluntly, she no longer wants to marry me,' Pierce explained with exaggerated patience.

'Oh, not that! I understand what you're saying—but *why*?'

How could anyone in their right mind, having once accepted Pierce's proposal, be fool enough to change her mind?

'She's found someone else.' The bitterness in the declaration made her wince painfully. 'Someone she met on the cruise—she prefers him.'

'Oh, Pierce...'

Impulsively Natalie took a step towards him, the instinct to comfort overwhelming, but she froze immediately, seeing the way he stiffened, his face closing up, warning her to stay away.

'How about that coffee?' he prompted.

'Oh, yes.'

She was glad to move away, into the kitchen, grateful for the chance to hide the pain she knew must show in her eyes. There was no way she could conceal it; just for that second she didn't have the strength to hold it back. The very matter-of-factness of his tone had told her only too plainly that he didn't want her sympathy, her concern. If he had slapped her hard in the face he couldn't have got the message across more clearly or more painfully. But she couldn't just leave it...

She turned to see Pierce lounging in the doorway.

'It must have hurt you.' If she wanted an idea of how it had felt, she had only to think of the pain she had experienced on hearing that he was to marry. Knowing it must happen some time hadn't made it any easier to bear.

'My ego suffered one hell of a shock, that's for sure.' Pierce's laughter was harsh, no trace of humour in it. 'And my pride.'

'Do you want to talk about it?' Natalie was filling the kettle as she spoke, concentrating fiercely on what she was doing. 'I mean, it might help.'

'No.' The declaration was hard and unyielding, leaving no room for negotiation. 'I don't want to talk about Phillippa, or her reasoning, or my feelings—I'd much rather talk about you.'

'Me?' Natalie set the mug she was holding down on the worktop with a crash that revealed her sense of shock. 'There's nothing interesting about me.'

'I beg to differ.' Pierce settled himself at the table. 'For one thing, you're not at all as I remember—you've changed.'

'Hardly surprising when you consider that it's almost three years since you saw me. It'd be pretty strange if I hadn't altered in some way in that time. I grew up, Pierce—I'm not a little girl any more.'

'You're certainly not,' he agreed. 'But there's more to it than that.'

'You mean I'm no longer the plain, scrawny teenager who used to hang around the Manor kitchens?' And who had been foolish enough to let herself believe—dream—that the occasional word or glance he tossed her way meant more than a casual interest in the daughter of one of the family's employees.

'No one could describe you as plain any more—you've flowered. Though you do yourself no favours scraping your hair back into that appalling spinster's bun.'

'I *am* a spinster, Pierce.'

It was an effort to speak because it was only then, belatedly, that Natalie paused to consider the possible implications of Pierce's blunt announcement for herself, common sense warning her to take things very carefully.

All those years ago, she would have given anything she possessed for just one word of approval, one compliment from him. Now, when he seemed prepared to give them out with a generous hand, she didn't know how to deal with it, the question of just what his motives were for being here permanently at the back of her thoughts, setting her mind on edge. After all, he had said that he wanted to talk about his broken engagement, but had then dismissed the subject immediately.

'Technically, I suppose you are, but I'm sure the term doesn't really apply—not after three years at college.'

'I'm an old-fashioned girl.' Natalie could feel the colour rush into her cheeks as she spoke.

His snort of dismissive laughter was disturbing.

'Not that old-fashioned, I'll bet! You're not trying to tell me you didn't have a long line of suitors forming a queue outside your door?'

'Hardly a line.'

'There must have been someone. You're not telling me that you spent three years at college and no one even asked you out. What were they all? Zombies?'

'Nothing like that.' Natalie's laughter was close to being genuine, only a little exaggerated in order to ease the tension that still hung in the air. 'But there was no one special.'

How could there have been, when the man she loved most in all the world was sitting opposite her right now, so close that all she had to do was reach out a hand and she could touch him, stroke his cheek, brush back the lock of silky black hair that had fallen over his forehead—?

Becoming aware of the way that Pierce was watching her, the disturbing intensity of that sapphire-blue gaze, she dragged herself back to reality with an effort.

'But you're not claiming that no one got a look-in?'

'If by "a look-in" you mean did any of them move in with me or vice versa, then no!'

Natalie stirred the coffee she had made with unnecessary force, before placing the mug on the table beside him, hoping that the jerky movement conveyed more indignation than the uneasy churning in the pit of her stomach she was actually feeling.

'Why are you harping on about this? I told you I was an old-fashioned sort of girl.'

'I'm not harping, just interested—and that's not so much old-fashioned as positively puritanical.' Pierce laughed. 'Are you trying to claim that you were waiting for Mr Right to come along?' He sounded frankly incredulous, a deeply sardonic amusement lacing his tone.

But what he had said was just a bit too close to the truth for comfort. Belatedly, Natalie realised that instead of damping down his curiosity she was in fact fanning its flames with her attempts to dodge his questions.

'Oh, all right, there *was* one man—Gerry. We were—close all the time I was at college.'

Gerry wouldn't mind his name being taken in vain. He had wanted to be more to her than a friend. In fact, they had shared several very pleasant evenings which, for his part, he might have thought would lead to greater things, but which to Natalie were simply that—enjoyable nights out with an attractive man as her escort. The light-hearted kisses she had given him had remained totally uninvolved, sparking off none of the disturbing sensations that Pierce's lightest touch could arouse.

'I thought there must have been—when do you see him?'

'I don't.' It might have been safer to pretend to an ongoing, passionate relationship with Gerry, but she couldn't do it. 'When we left Sheffield he got a job in Edinburgh.'

'And it's not a case of absence making the heart grow fonder?'

'More like out of sight, out of mind, though we do write occasionally.'

'Very occasionally, from the sound of your voice,' Pierce murmured. 'Whatever your Gerry did, it certainly riled you.'

'It's not what *he* did—it's what *you're* doing.'

'Me?' Pierce froze, his mug half raised, his look of confusion so apparently uncontrived that Natalie could almost believe it was genuine.

'Yes, you—you're prying into my private life.' The knowledge of how dangerously close he had come to the truth made her voice tart. 'Asking too many questions.'

'The privilege isn't exclusive,' Pierce returned, surprising her. 'You can ask as well as answer. Oh, come on, Nat!' he laughed when she looked distinctly sceptical. 'This isn't the girl I know and love! As I recall, the problem used to be shutting you up rather than getting you to talk.'

'And I can ask *anything*?' Natalie asked with only a tiny shake in her voice. Her peace of mind demanded that she try to ignore that 'I know and love', being only too well aware of just how cynically it was meant.

'Anything within reason.'

'Then why did you decide to get married?'

The question was so close to the surface of her mind that it burst from her before she had time to consider whether it was really wise, but at least she had enough presence of mind to catch herself up in time and not add the name that would have revealed that what she really wanted to ask was 'Why did you want to marry *Phillippa*?'

But she'd overstepped the mark this time; she knew it as she saw the way that his face closed up, his mouth hardening, the muscles in his jaw tightening.

'It's all right! I shouldn't—'

'You asked—I'll answer. After all—' Pierce's laugh was a travesty of genuine humour, no warmth in it at all '—after what's happened, it would probably be a good idea to have a look at my motives—see exactly how I got myself into this mess.'

If she had regretted the question moments before, then now she wished she had cut her tongue out—anything other than push him into this darkly cynical frame of mind which made her want to weep for the loss of the ease they had shared only a short time before.

'I always wanted to get married—'

'It looked that way!' Natalie couldn't help retorting, recalling the seemingly endless stream of girlfriends that had blighted her adolescence.

'Oh, damn it, Nat! Don't look so sceptical! What's wrong with playing the field until you find the right person—the one you want to settle down with?'

'Nothing,' she was forced to mutter, incapable of injecting any enthusiasm into the word, being only too painfully aware of the fact that Pierce believed he had found 'the right person' in Phillippa. 'But I don't know about field—it was more like fields—acres of them,' she added in an attempt to conceal her private pain.

'But I never led anyone on, let them think it was serious when it was nothing of the sort. Every girl I ever dated knew exactly where she stood—that there was no commitment—just a lot of fun. They all had a good time, and so did I—you know how it is.'

Natalie managed an inarticulate murmur that she hoped he would take as agreement. She wished she did know how it was. She had tried dating for fun, both at school and, later, at college, and she had enjoyed the company of the men she'd gone out with—some more than others—but that was all, and in the end it had all been ultimately disappointing.

'No?' She hadn't convinced him.

'I have to admit that I find no-commitment relationships rather like just treading water—not going anywhere and so frustratingly unproductive. I'm afraid I'm an all or nothing sort of person.'

And Pierce was all she wanted, but she couldn't have him and so would she have to settle for nothing?

'You always were far too serious for your own good. It was never like that for me—until my father died.'

Pierce stared down into the coffee in his mug, a frown drawing his dark, straight brows together.

'Then I came up hard against a terrible realisation of my own mortality—one that was enhanced by a strong sense of responsibility.'

'Responsibility?'

'Like my dad, I'd always wanted children, but suddenly that need was overlaid by the realisation that the Donellan line depended on me. The Manor has been in our family for centuries and I know Dad wanted it to continue that way— I want it too. I suppose that sounds positively feudal to you.'

'Not really.'

Natalie chose her words with care, painfully aware of the flatness of his voice on that 'I'd always wanted children'. He'd wanted a family and now, because of Phillippa's decision, he would be denied that. He sounded as if he had lost sight of all his dreams.

'I think I, more than most, can understand how you feel. After all, growing up without a father, never even knowing who he was, has always made me feel incomplete somehow—as if some important piece of my own personal jigsaw puzzle is missing, one that would help me see the complete picture.'

'Your mother never said anything, even at the end?'

'She wasn't capable of saying anything,' Natalie sighed, her eyes clouding at the painful memory of her mother's last illness, three years before, while she had been in her final year at college. 'At least, not coherently, though there was one point when she kept saying a name over and over—Hilton—I think it was that. I've let myself believe that it was my father's surname, and that, at the end, she forgave him for abandoning her.'

Her voice had no strength to it, her thoughts swinging to the irony in the way that, while in full health her mother had been so determined to keep the two of them apart, her illness had in fact brought her and Pierce closer together, if only briefly.

Because if she hadn't already fallen head over heels in love with Pierce, then she would have done so on that bleak March morning when he had arrived out of the blue with the appalling news of Nora Brennan's collapse. If he hadn't already had possession of it, she would have given him her heart as a result of the unfailing kindness and consideration he had shown her then and throughout the dark days that had followed. Certainly, it had been the time when her love had matured, becoming that of a woman instead of the girl Pierce had known.

'It would mean so much to you?'

'It would help me feel I know who I really am—if you know what I mean. If I could just know who my father was, even if he's dead, at least then I'd have a name to put on my birth certificate instead of that empty space. It'd go a little way to make up for not having a real family. So, you see, I can appreciate how important your family name must be to you and that you'd want that line to continue. And, of course, I expect your mother would want grandchildren.'

'My mother—' Pierce's face darkened, his mouth twisting in the firelight. 'There's going to be hell to pay there—she's already bought a particularly spectacular hat in anticipation of the wedding that isn't going to be.'

The wry humour didn't convince; Natalie was still very much aware of the bitterness underneath.

'She doesn't know?'

'No one knows except for Phillippa and myself—and now you.'

'I won't tell anyone,' Natalie put in hastily, and was surprised by his dismissive shrug.

'People will have to know some time. It might as well be sooner rather than later.'

'Your mother won't be the only one who'll be disappointed. Everyone in the village was looking forward to a summer wedding—'

'Hell and damnation, Nat!' Pierce's furious roar was matched by a violent movement that brought him swiftly to his feet, so that he towered over her, the ominous threat of his dark scowl making her nerves twist in fearful apprehension. 'My marriage wasn't planned to please the bloody village!'

Too late, Natalie realised the tactlessness of her words. Pierce had always hated the almost possessive way in which the inhabitants of Ellerby regarded the Donellans. The family were still seen very much as the local nobility, their lives and activities commented on with almost as much interest as the royal family was nationally.

'Of course not— I'm sorry, I didn't think.'

Her shaken words seemed to pull him back from wherever his savage thoughts had taken him, leaving him looking troubled and, just for a moment, strangely confused. At last his eyes focused on her again, taking in the way she had shrunk back from him, her wide, dark eyes.

'Oh, hell, Nat—I'm sorry.' Roughly he raked both hands through his black hair, disturbing its shining sleekness. 'I should never have come—never have inflicted myself on you like this. I'm not fit company for anyone.'

'That's hardly surprising in the circumstances.' Natalie switched on a smile that she hoped looked genuine. 'And you didn't *inflict* yourself.'

'Nevertheless, I ought to go.'

He was looking around him for his jacket and something about the way he moved, the angle at which he held his head alerted her, sounding warning bells in her thoughts.

'Pierce . . .'

'Mmm?'

The heavy lids hooding the over-bright eyes he turned confirmed her suspicions, as did a faint slowness in his reaction. It was tiny, almost imperceptible, and only someone as sensitive to everything about him as she was would have noticed it.

'How much *have* you had to drink?'

'Too much to remember clearly, but not enough to make me forget,' he returned with a sudden harshness that she had to ignore as she moved to catch hold of his arm.

'You had something before you came here, didn't you? And then the sherry—Pierce, you shouldn't have been driving in that state!'

'My dear Natalie—my eminently *sensible* little friend—how very moral and controlled you are about everything.'

Those sapphire eyes danced in unholy amusement as Pierce lifted one hand and rested it lightly against her cheek. But a moment later his mood changed again, sobering abruptly as he shrugged off her protest.

'I know I would have done better not to drive, but I wasn't over the limit, and I had to talk to someone or go out of my mind.'

'Yes—but all the same...' Natalie struggled to ignore the warmth that had flooded through her veins at his touch, and the double-edged effect of that 'little friend'. 'You can't drive any further tonight.'

'I have to, sweetheart—unless you have some alternative to suggest.'

Sweetheart! If anything convinced her that he was not completely sober, it was that. Pierce had never called her anything even remotely so affectionate before. In the past he had labelled her only by the shortened form of her name, refusing to use its full version because 'Natalie's far too elegant for a little scrap like you'. Such uncharacteristic behaviour was more revealing than anything that had gone before.

There was only one possibility. 'You'll have to stay here.'

'Here?'

Black eyebrows lifted in an exaggerated expression of amazement, and the gleam of wicked humour lit up those blue eyes once again.

'That's a highly improper suggestion, Miss Brennan.' The sardonic mockery did nothing to hide the cutting edge to his words. 'Whatever will the neighbours think?'

'They needn't know anything about it.' Natalie refused to rise to his taunt. 'After all, you said that you parked the car some distance away, and if you leave latish tomorrow when everyone's gone to work—' She broke off on a stab of pain as Pierce shook his head in adamant rejection.

'I think not,' he said curtly. 'My coat—'

'*No*, Pierce.'

Moving swiftly, she reached the jacket before him, snatching it up and holding it behind her back, out of his reach.

'I won't let you—you're not fit to drive.'

'Then I'll walk.' His tone was positively dangerous now, his eyes almost black with anger, resistance and denial of her arguments stamped into every line of his body. 'I can't be found drunk in charge of my feet!'

'It's pouring with rain! You'll get soaked!'

'I won't melt. Natalie, I can't stay—I can't share your—'

'You won't have to *share* anything!'

Concentrating hard on getting him to listen to reason, she knew she shouldn't pause to consider how his words made her feel. She couldn't cope with the ambiguous feelings that assailed her at the thought that he actually believed she was offering him a place in her own bed, the realisation that this was the only possibility that had crossed his mind. In her thoughts she could hear her mother's voice, cynical conviction in every word.

'There's only one thing a man like that wants from a girl like you, and I don't have to tell you what that is.'

And of course she could have no doubt as to what was meant when she herself was the living proof of that 'one thing' a man might want, and even more evidence of the fact that when it became plain that that pleasure would result in consequences then the man responsible wouldn't be seen for dust.

But her mother had been wrong about Pierce, as Natalie knew to her cost. *He* had made it plain that even when it was offered he had no interest at all in her body. So now, squashing down the pain that simply remembering brought, Natalie had no hesitation in pursuing her point determinedly.

'This may not be the Manor House, but I do have a perfectly adequate spare bedroom.'

'All the same—'

He made a move towards the door, but Natalie was there before him, slamming it shut and putting her back against it so that he would have to move her physically out of the way if he was really determined to leave.

'Natalie—'

'No argument, Pierce!'

She had to struggle to ignore the warning implicit in his use of her full name, refusing to let herself consider the fact that his determination to leave was motivated by much more than a simple concern for her reputation. Allowing herself the thought that he simply didn't want to stay *with her* would weaken her too much and she couldn't give in now.

'I couldn't have it on my conscience if I let you go and you hurt yourself or someone—'

'For God's sake, woman!'

As hard fingers closed over her arms, digging fiercely into the soft flesh, she knew with a terrible sinking sense of despair that if he did decide to move her she would be unable to resist, even her determination appearing pathetically puny when compared with his muscular strength.

And in the same moment she suddenly, shockingly, but far, far too late, knew a dreadful creeping fear at the thought of the force of the anger she had awoken in Pierce, the power she had unthinkingly released and might be totally incapable of stopping. She had always known that Pierce Donellan was a formidable force to be reckoned with, both at home and in the business world. The respect his estate workers had for him, his almost legendary reputation as a big fish in a very big pool were well known, but never before had she had that forcefulness turned on her personally, and, faced with the storm power of it, she needed all her courage in order to hold her ground.

'I can't let you do this!'

For a frightening second his grip tightened bruisingly, and she swallowed hard, nerving herself for the inevitable. Surprisingly, it didn't come. Instead, Pierce looked deep into her eyes, seeing the determination in their coffee-coloured depths—the defiance—the fear.

'Oh, hell!' he muttered harshly, releasing her with such abruptness that she stumbled backwards and would actually have fallen if it hadn't been for the support of the door behind her. 'All right, if it'll get you off my back— you win! Which room?'

'Top of the stairs, first right—bathroom's just next door.'

Natalie could feel no pleasure in her victory. Did he have to make it so obvious that staying was the last thing he wanted? she asked herself as Pierce, after the curtest of goodnights, made his way upstairs. She had got what she wanted, but at the cost of a painful blow to her heart.

She would give him time to use the bathroom and get into bed, she told herself, determinedly turning her attention to washing up, and refusing to let her mind drift because it showed an alarming tendency to wander off on to disturbing thoughts of Pierce undressing in the soft blue and white bedroom, of his strong, lean body sliding between the sheets...

'Put the milk bottle out—lock the door—bolt it—fireguard—switch off the lights...' she muttered to herself in order to provide a distraction from the wayward path her thoughts were taking. Was twenty minutes long enough?

It would have to be. It was coming up to midnight; she was worn out, and she had to be up before seven in the morning.

Not that she had any real hope of sleeping, she told herself as, dressed in a short denim-blue cotton night-dress, she brushed her teeth before taking herself off to bed. The thought of Pierce in the room directly opposite her own was more than enough to keep her wide awake. She would be able to hear every creak of the elderly bed, any slight movement he made.

Stop it!

Ruthlessly she splashed her face with cold water, praying that it would cool her heated thoughts, lower the heightened temperature that was the result of her crazily racing pulse. It was as she dried herself that she realised she hadn't provided clean towels for Pierce. She had been so knocked back by his unexpected capitulation that she hadn't even thought about it. He would need them in the morning.

She would just drop them in on her way back to her room. He was probably already fast asleep anyway, the wine he had drunk having taken effect, but when, finding his door ajar, she put her head round it, she was surprised to see that the bedside lamp was still on, throwing a pool of warm light onto the dark head that lay on the crisp white pillows.

But Pierce's eyes were closed, she noted with a sense of relief, his long black lashes lying like crescents just above the strong cheekbones, the dark regrowth of his beard already shadowing the hard line of his jaw. She'd just leave the towels and go, she told herself, moving on tiptoe so as not to disturb him.

It was as she reached for the switch to turn off the lamp that those heavy lashes lifted slowly and she froze, staring straight into slightly unfocused, sleep-clouded sapphire-blue eyes.

'Natalie...' Her name was a weary sigh rather than a sound of welcome, stilling the tentative smile on her lips. 'What the hell do you want now?'

'I just brought some towels—I forgot to give them to you earlier.' Pain made her voice tight and cold, her gesture jerky as she indicated the small bundle at the foot of the bed. 'I thought you'd probably want a shower in the morning.'

'Thanks.'

She was dismissed, his indifferent tone said. His eyes were closing again, deliberately, she thought, communicating only too clearly the message that she was not wanted.

'All right, then, I'll leave you in peace.'

'Please do.'

Those two words burned like bitter acid in her heart.

'Well...goodnight.'

She couldn't help herself; a shadow of her distress tinged her words in spite of the effort she made to hold it back, and, as he heard it, Pierce's eyes flew open again.

'Nat...' His voice was low and strangely rough at the edges. 'Thanks for everything.'

There was a subtle, indefinable change in his face, one she couldn't even begin to interpret, and suddenly he lifted himself up on the pillows, holding out a hand to her.

'I don't know what I'd have done if you hadn't been at home.'

'I'm glad I was here for you.'

She tried to sound brisk and matter-of-fact, fighting against the recollection of just why he was here in the first place—because of the hurt that another woman had inflicted on him. But, try as she might, she wasn't strong enough to resist the appeal of that outstretched hand, the new softness in his eyes.

Her heart jerked violently in her chest as she perched awkwardly on the side of the bed, taking the warm strength of his fingers in hers.

'After all, isn't that what friends are for?' She let her hand linger in his for a moment longer, then forced herself to make a move to get up. 'Now you must get some sleep—I need some if you don't; I have—'

'Nat,' Pierce interrupted suddenly, his voice touched with a rawly urgent note that stilled her, holding her unable to move. 'Don't go—I don't want to be alone—not tonight.'

'But...' Looking into his eyes, she saw how they had darkened, only the tiniest trace of blue edging the blackness of the pupils. 'Pierce—'

'Please.'

It was frightening how easily she found herself considering it, appalling how little hesitation there was before she accepted the idea. It was downright impossible to say no, even though stern reason warned her not to consider the idea even for a second, but to get out *now*.

'I don't have any ulterior motives.' Slight as it had been, Pierce had caught her hesitation and hurried to reassure her. 'For one thing, I'm half asleep already— I was dead on my feet downstairs—and I've really had far too much to drink to be considered a threat to any woman. And besides, we're friends...'

If only he knew how much she had come to hate that word, particularly now, when the description seemed so very far from flattering. It was more than he had ever offered her before, but a million miles from what she wanted. As his *friend*, she had no physical appeal for him. The cold rationality of that thought pushed her into a belated attempt to assert some sort of control over things.

'I don't think it would be—'

'*Please.*'

It came so softly that she might have missed it if she hadn't been so sensitive to everything about him, but she did catch it and it tugged at her already vulnerable heart. It would have taken a far stronger will than she possessed to resist that low-voiced appeal, and besides, he was already drifting away into exhausted sleep, heavy lids closing, his breathing slowing.

Looking at him now, with those brilliant eyes hidden from her, his face relaxing from the taut, strained lines that had drawn the skin tight over his forceful bone structure, she could see the younger Pierce in him again.

'I need a hand to hold...'

'What?' She couldn't believe she had heard right, the words slurred with sleep. Or, if she had, did it mean as much to him as it did to her?

'A hand to hold . . .'

Natalie bit down hard on her lower lip as the intervening years were stripped away and she was once more a skinny adolescent, physically a late developer and desperately, painfully self-conscious, particularly when Pierce Donellan was around.

He hadn't noticed her at first, of course. When her mother had started work at the Manor, she had been a mere eleven, and Pierce a lordly twenty-year-old. He had barely spared her a glance then, or at any point over the next couple of years, but then fate had stepped in in a dramatic way, throwing her quite literally at his feet.

She had been on her way home from school, returning late after staying for choir practice, and already the gathering dusk had been closing in around her, the conditions worsened by a miserable, persistent drizzle. It had been as she was crossing the road to the bus-stop that a motor cyclist, travelling far too fast, had come roaring round the corner, slamming into her and sending her flying. For a moment she had lost consciousness, coming round a short time later to find herself lying on the pavement supported by strong, comforting arms and with a pair of deeply concerned blue eyes looking down into hers.

She'd thought she'd died and gone to heaven, she recalled now, a soft smile curving her lips at the memory of the way Pierce, who had been taking that route home when he had seen the accident, had despatched someone to collect her mother while he stayed with her, travelling to the hospital in the ambulance when it came. He had held her hand, soothed away her fear with gentle words, and hadn't even noticed the way her badly grazed arm had dripped blood all over his expensive suit.

She'd lost her heart to him then, and in the weeks that followed, when, knowing that a fractured ankle meant that she was confined to her room in the housekeeper's quarters at the Manor, he had been a frequent visitor, bringing books and games to keep her amused, tasty treats to tempt her appetite. She had lost her heart completely and had never, ever been able to get it back.

It had been then that, unable to thank him properly, but wanting to convey her gratitude as well as she could, she had poured out the ardent, if naïve, declaration of feeling that Pierce's words had brought so vividly to mind.

'If ever you need me—for anything—you only have to ask,' she had said, not pausing to ask herself what an unsophisticated, barely fourteen-year-old could possibly offer to a grown man almost a decade older. 'If you need someone—a hand to hold as you held mine—I'll be there.'

But then, of course, what she had felt for Pierce had been simple hero-worship, the blind, unquestioning devotion of innocence, uncomplicated by the sort of considerations that had come with maturity and a greater understanding of the complexities of relationships between men and women. With young adulthood had come a realisation of exactly what her mother feared, and a new sense of awareness—the sort of awareness that now kept her frozen on the edge of the bed, unable to move one way or the other.

'Nat?' Pierce forced open sleep-blurred eyes, their jewel brightness softened to the gentleness of a spring morning sky. 'I just need someone...'

Letting her breath escape on a soundless sigh, Natalie admitted to herself that there was no way she could hold out any longer. If all he wanted from her was the sort of uncomplicated friendship he had offered all those years before, then that was what she would give him.

Besides, she knew that she was incapable of resisting the temptation to finally be able to be closer to him, physically at least, than she had ever been before, to hold him against her, just this once, offering what comfort she could until he fell asleep and was too deeply unconscious to be aware of her slipping from his side and returning to her own bed.

Just this once, she told herself as she lifted the corner of the blankets and slid in beside him. What harm could it do?

CHAPTER THREE

FROM the first second, Natalie knew she had made a terrible mistake.

She had promised herself that she would simply wait until Pierce was deeply asleep, and then she would go, but in the moment that she felt the warm length of his strong body against hers it was as if the heat of his skin had seeped into every cell in her body, softening bone and muscle and draining her of any strength, any ability to move.

Each time her mind told her that she should go, that Pierce was oblivious to her presence, that there was no way he would notice if she left, she found that her limbs had no strength to move, that they were weighed down by a sensual lassitude that had nothing to do with any concern about disturbing the man at her side.

Just one more minute, she told herself, glorying in the soft warmth of his breath on her neck, the slide of the black silk of his hair against her cheek. One of her arms lay around his shoulders, tinglingly aware of the power of the muscles under the satin skin, the rough texture of the dark, curling hair on his chest, and it was all that she could do to stop her fingers from wandering further, exploring the lean strength so close to her, the long legs touching her own.

Just one more minute; that was all she wanted. One more minute to lie like this, drawing in the musky male scent of his body, hearing the faint sound of his breathing, feeling the way his chest rose and fell. This might be all she would ever have of him, all she would ever know of the physical pleasure of being close. It was probably her one and only chance ever to hold him, and the memories she was storing up tonight would have to last her for the rest of her life.

Just one more minute...

She wasn't aware of falling asleep, knew nothing more until, some time in the dark stillness of the night, she stirred at last, surfacing slowly to become conscious of some restriction to her movement, instinctively tensing against it, straining to be free, then freezing again as the warm restraint tightened, holding her still.

'No,' said a voice in her ear, the lazy drawl having an unyielding edge to it that sent a shiver of apprehension running down her spine. 'Stay right where you are.'

Pierce's voice, and Pierce's arms were holding her captive.

'But—' Her throat was dry, making her voice weak and croaking.

'Shh.'

It shivered across her skin, making her twist in uncontrollable response, a small cry of shock escaping her as the unwary movement brought her slender legs into intimate contact with the hair-roughened length of his. The next moment, that cry was cut short by the soft pressure of Pierce's mouth on hers in a swift, gentle caress that made all her senses spring to life, knotting her nerves with the immediate intensity of her response.

'This is nice—very nice indeed.'

In the dim light, Natalie could see that Pierce's eyes were barely open, and the dreamy, unfocused sound of his voice made her heart skip a beat at the thought that perhaps he wasn't really awake, that possibly he was still tangled in dreams, thinking she was someone else—and there was only one person that could be.

She didn't know what would happen, what, if anything, might result from the situation in which she now found herself, but she was sure of one thing. She couldn't bear to be mistaken for the fiancée Pierce had loved and lost; it would tear her heart into pieces.

'Pierce...'

What little there was of her voice died in her throat as his hands moved over her, stroking, moulding the shape of her body under the soft cotton of her nightdress, lingering heart-stoppingly at her breasts and hips.

'You never used to feel like this before.' His voice was still blurred and thick.

'That was because we never used to do this sort of thing.'

'How very foolish,' Pierce murmured. 'Foolish—and very wasteful.'

'Pierce...' Natalie tried again.

'We should have, you know.' His lips were on hers, the words whispered against the softness of her mouth. 'Should have done this a long time ago. We've wasted an appalling amount of time, you and I.'

Trying to control her reactions didn't work. Already her wayward body was responding, opening to him like a flower to the sun. As she moved against him, she felt the force of his desire pressing into the softness of her stomach, triggering a heated reaction deep inside her.

She was weakening—no, not *weakening*—she had never had the strength to resist Pierce from the start. This was why she had always kept her distance physically—because she had known from the outset, from the moment that that searing sexual awareness had burned away her innocent hero-worship, replacing it with something much more complex and dangerous, that if he was ever to touch her it would be like this. She had known she would never be able to fight him—and she couldn't now—but she couldn't have any doubts—she had to know for certain.

'Are you sure?'

'Never been surer,' that husky voice assured her. 'We wasted a lot of time in the past, but not now...'

Warm lips slid up the pale length of her throat, across her cheek, capturing her mouth again in the same moment that his caressing hands reached the hem of the blue nightdress, easing it upwards, his fingers burning a scorching path to the aching sensitivity of her breasts. When he moulded them softly, the heat of his palms against her skin made her writhe in unrestrained delight.

'You used to be such a little girl—but now you're all woman.'

Natalie drew in her breath in sharp delight, her back arching in immediate response as the soft warmth of his hands closed over her sensitised flesh, sending shafts of pleasure through her whole body, heating the blood in her veins.

'The sort of woman any man would want...' The words were punctuated by tiny, sharply teasing bites that made her lower body jerk in instinctive response. 'And here you are—with me...'

'Pierce...'

She wasn't even aware of whether she had actually formed his name as a coherent sound, knowing only that she was sinking deeper and deeper, hot waters of desire closing over her head, very definitely going down for the third time—and yet she *had* to know.

'Pierce—'

'Hush, Natalie,' that soft voice soothed, and at the sound of her own name every nerve in her body clenched on a wave of pure joy.

He *knew*. Pierce had spoken her name so that she could be in no doubt that he knew very clearly just who she was. She needed no further convincing that it was her—Natalie—and not Phillippa he was making love to. She knew it, and, more importantly, Pierce knew it too, the thought bringing such a rush of happiness that only physical action could express it.

And so, acting on instincts she hadn't known she possessed, instincts that must have been inherent in her as a woman, handed down from the dawn of time, from Eve herself, because she certainly had no experience on which to base them, she reached for Pierce, linking her hands in the soft hair at the nape of his neck and pulling his head down towards hers so that their mouths met.

The explosion of need deep within her was instantaneous, softening her lips under his, opening them to the thrust of his tongue, bringing her body close to his like a needle drawn irresistibly to a magnet, the feel of the hard muscle, the roughness of hair strangely alien and yet somehow so perfectly right that she sighed against his mouth—a small, satisfied sound.

It was as if an electrical storm was brewing, charging the atmosphere with powerful currents, striking sparks from Pierce's hands where he touched, from his mouth where it pressed against her skin. She was adrift, unable to think, knowing only that this was what she had wanted for so long, and she couldn't believe it was real.

'Don't be shy, Natalie.' Pierce's voice was husky in her ear. 'Relax, darling—touch me.'

'Touch me'! She felt as if she had been given the key that would unlock the chains that held her, binding her to the earth. To have the freedom to touch him, caress him, kiss him, was all she had ever wanted, and now he had given it to her, not even knowing how much it meant. She felt as if she was soaring, floating high up into a golden sky where the heat of the sun warmed her blood, driving away all caution, all restraint.

'Like this?'

Her fingers gloried in the feel of him, the warmth of his skin, the power of hard muscle underneath. She let them wander where they wanted, down the long back, over the narrow hips, smiling secretly to herself as he jerked convulsively under her touch.

'Yes, like that— Oh, yes! But— Oh, God, *Nat*!'

Hard fingers gripped her shoulders, pulling her underneath him, his breathing ragged and uneven, and she felt a faint whisper of fear across her skin, just for a second. But then he kissed her again, muttering her name against her lips, and all tension vanished. This was Pierce—the man she had loved for so long. And *this* was what she had wanted—for ever, it seemed.

But however much she wanted it there was still the sharp stab of pain that clenched her muscles involuntarily against the hard force of his invasion, her tension and the small cry she couldn't hold back stilling him at once to stare down at her shadowed face.

'Natalie,' he said unsteadily. 'Nat...?'

'No!' She was suddenly fearful that he would stop, that, recognising her inexperience, he would no longer want her as he had just moments before. 'Don't stop.'

'But Nat—'

'I said, don't stop!'

Instinct came to her aid, relaxing the muscles that had tightened, making her move slightly under him, awkwardly at first, but then more sensually, more confidently, as an inner, intuitive rhythm took control.

'Natalie—'

Her name was a shaken cry, choked off as she kissed the protest from his lips, stroking her hands across his skin, down over the powerful ribcage, sliding them round the narrow waist, slipping lower...

'Nat—sweetheart—don't—I can't—'

The husky desperation in Pierce's voice went straight to her head like a glass of the most potent spirit, combining with the soft tug of his mouth at her breast to send her soaring into a world of delight such as she had never known before. She had never felt so free, so sure—so *alive*. Every move was made without thinking, every caress a delight, and somewhere ahead, like the light at the end of a tunnel, was something...

She was reaching—reaching for it—when suddenly, far sooner than she had anticipated, and well before she was emotionally ready, she felt the world explode around her in a shower of stars. A moment later Pierce gave a sharp cry, his whole body tightened and he crushed her hard against him, his arms like bands of steel, until, slowly, he subsided against her, his breathing ragged and uneven.

Coming back to reality slowly and painfully, Natalie was only aware of one thought in her mind, like a nagging ache through the glow of fulfilment.

It was over. That brief moment of delight was all she would ever know of Pierce's love. No—not his love, because for him it had only been a way of holding back the darkness, filling the emptiness for a short time. But for her it had been the magic of giving herself to the man who had held her heart in his hands for so many years, and now, too soon—far, far too soon—it was over. In spite of herself, she couldn't hold back a faint sigh of regret, tears burning her eyes.

'Oh, God, Nat—I'm sorry.' To her distress, Pierce had caught the slight sound.

'No.' She closed his mouth with her fingers. 'Pierce— *please*!'

She didn't want him to talk; didn't want any recriminations, any post-mortems.

'Damn it, this wasn't how I meant it to be,' he muttered against her hand, but even through the anger she could hear how exhaustion was blurring his voice again, the stress of the day, the long journey, and the effects of the wine he had drunk, claiming him again even though he was trying so hard to fight them.

'I know.'

Once more, instinct came to her aid, driving her to lift her hands to his hair, smoothing, stroking gently, feeling the tension in the powerful body ease slowly, like the tide ebbing away from the shore.

'I know—but it doesn't matter. It's not important.'

What mattered—all that really mattered to her—was that just this once, for one brief moment at least, he had wanted *her*, and no one else, and, knowing that, how could she ever say that what had happened had been wrong in any way, or ever regret it?

Beside her, Pierce sighed deeply, losing the battle to keep his heavy lids from closing, his muscled frame relaxing as he slid into sleep, and a small, sad smile curled her lips. He had wanted her, but not enough. Enough for tonight, perhaps, but not for the lifetime commitment she dreamed of.

'Next time...'

The words were just a breath, long-drawn-out and barely audible, oblivion claiming Pierce even as he tried to form them.

Next time, echoed inside Natalie's head, the ache behind her eyes finally breaking into the weak, desolated tears she could no longer hold back. *Next time—* but there would be no next time; she knew that.

Pierce had turned to her in a moment of depression, knocked off balance by the loneliness brought on by the loss of the woman he had wanted to marry, and nothing more. That was all that tonight had meant. He had wanted her only as some warmly willing companion who would hold back the darkness for a while, help ease the raw pain in his heart, fill the aching gap where Phillippa should have been—but at least he had known who she was and, for that moment, had wanted *her*.

But there could never, ever be any future in it. In the cold light of morning, he would see what had happened as the mistake it was, see it and probably feel terrible about it. He would be so angry at himself that perhaps he wouldn't know how to face her.

Well, she could spare him that. She *had* to, she told herself, forcing back her tears with fierce determination. If she didn't, then very likely she would lose him more effectively than before. And if she spared Pierce that embarrassment, then she would also spare herself. So, in the morning—

In the morning. As the words hit home inside her head, reality came with them, forcing her to register the growing light beyond the window, to acknowledge that, far from being some hours in the future, the morning was here, now, and she was quite unprepared to face it. Deep inside, she knew what had to be done—that she had no choice, even if her already aching heart cried out in protest at the further injuries she was inflicting on it.

'Goodbye, my love.'

She formed the words silently, not even daring to whisper them for fear of breaking into the sleep that held Pierce unconscious at her side, knowing that she couldn't risk one last kiss, however much she longed to press her lips against his shadowed cheek. Moving painfully slowly, taking infinite care, she eased herself away from him, cradling his head in her hands until she could lower it gently to the pillow.

But even though every movement seemed to be made in slow motion there was still one terrible, heart-wrenching moment when, as his cheek touched the cool softness of the cotton covers, he stirred, his eyelids fluttering, long, dark lashes lifting very slightly.

'Nat?' he murmured hazily, making her freeze in panic, her heart thudding painfully high up in her throat.

'It's all right.'

She had no idea how she got the words past the knot of emotion that threatened to choke her, drawing on strength she hadn't known she possessed in order to sound confident and yet soothing at the same time.

'It's all right. Just go back to sleep.'

The way he turned his face into the pillow, relaxing again at the sound of her voice, tore at her heart with its unexpected vulnerability.

She even lifted her hand to smooth back the tumble of black hair that had strayed forward over his face, her fingers almost touching him before she realised what she was doing. Immediately, she pulled back, fearful that he might waken, not knowing what would happen if he did.

As she waited, holding her breath, she couldn't stop her eyes from moving hungrily over his strong-boned features, stamping their imprint on her mind. Already it was over, the special night they had shared; even in his sleep he was already moving away from her. The memories she stored up now would have to last her for ever, she reminded herself, reluctantly acknowledging that it was safe to move.

It was only when she reached her own room and was able to check the clock that the full impact of reality dawned with the realisation that it was far later than she had thought. Thrown off balance by the events of the evening, she had forgotten to set her alarm, and as a result she would have to dash if she was going to be ready for work on time.

The frantic rush that ensued drove all other possible considerations from her mind, and it was only now, when she was actually at the door, her key in her hand, that she paused to consider what might happen when Pierce woke.

On one level, she could only be grateful for the fact that she hadn't had to face him, hadn't had to see the embarrassment, the regret that she knew must inevitably cloud his eyes, but, equally, she didn't want him to think *she* couldn't bear to face him. After all, they would probably have to meet again at some point, and it would be better to prepare the ground, allowing for some sort of civilised behaviour.

It took only seconds to scribble a hasty note, a little longer to consider where to put it so that Pierce would be sure to find it. In the end, she opted for the kitchen table—he would be certain to want a cup of coffee at least, before leaving. But still she found it hard to force herself out the door, reading the letter through once more, and then, with sudden inspiration, snatching up her pen again to add a final line.

'Goodbye, Pierce,' she whispered, dropping a kiss onto his name, printed on the outside of the folded paper. Now she would really have to run.

Her hasty dash for the bus left her with no time for second thoughts. She didn't even have a chance to glance back at the house and the bedroom window behind which Pierce still slept before they turned the corner and it was out of sight. It was better this way, she told herself. After all, there was no future in their relationship.

'Fares, please.' The conductor, red-nosed from the cold, glared at her in a way that told her without words that this was not his first attempt to bring her back from her abstracted state.

'Oh, I'm sorry.'

Fumbling in her purse for the right change, she realised with a nasty little jolt just how foolish she was being thinking this way.

There was no *relationship* to have a future anyway. A one-night stand was all it had been, with herself as stand-in for the woman Pierce had really wanted. At least by leaving in this way she had spared him the embarrassment of having to make that clear to her.

She wouldn't have been able to cope with that; wouldn't have been able to face him and see the distance that would come into his eyes, the way he would try not to hurt her, for courtesy's sake, if nothing else. That would have been more than she could bear, after the closeness they had shared.

Or, rather, the closeness *she* had felt. To Pierce it had been nothing more than the appeasing of a physical need, a way of holding back the darkness for a brief space of time. And that made it all the more painful to think that the glimpse of heaven she had had was all that she would ever know. But she also knew one other thing; brief and bitter-sweet as it had been, it was still an experience she would never forget.

CHAPTER FOUR

'Did you hear the latest about our Pierce?'

'Latest?'

Natalie had caught her friend's words with only half an ear, most of her attention concentrated on cramming the last of a bundle of papers into a battered cardboard box. She could only hope that the children's paintings would survive such rough handling—it was either that or have them ruined by the appalling weather conditions outside. But then the impact of what Sue had said hit home.

'What latest? And do you mean Pierce *Donellan*?'

She made an effort to control her voice, but all the same it shook betrayingly and she could only pray that Sue would believe her reaction to be the result of the struggle with the awkward mass of drawings. Surely the village grapevine couldn't have latched onto the news of the break-up of his engagement already?

'Who else? How many Pierces do you know?'

Only one, and that was enough, Natalie thought privately. Just the sound of his name had set her pulse racing, raising her colour and making her breathe rapidly and unevenly. Somehow she had struggled through the day on automatic pilot, barely able to concentrate on her teaching, most of her mind back in her home, with Pierce, wondering what he was doing, whether he had woken yet, how he had felt when he had found her gone...

'So what's happened?'

'Chris was up at the Manor during the holidays, and he heard all about the party they held in London to celebrate the engagement—dancing till dawn, and champagne flowing like water. Apparently the lucky lady's name is—'

'Phillippa,' Natalie put in flatly, not letting her eyes meet Sue's for fear that her friend might see the distress that had turned them from their usual rich warm brown to a near ebony bleakness.

She was glad of the chance to turn away, taking her serviceable beige trench coat from the hook by the door and pulling it on as she struggled with her inner feelings, with the pain that warred with a weak longing to tell someone what had happened, to confide in her friend in the hope that she could come to terms with what had happened.

'Of course, I was forgetting your links with the family meant you would know...'

'Mmm.'

Natalie pretended to be concentrating on smoothing her long, dark hair, tucking a couple of straying strands back into the neat coil at the nape of her neck, using the time to try to regain a little composure because in reality her dark-eyed gaze was unfocused, her heart-shaped face just a blur in the mirror before her.

It was funny, she reflected, just how possessive people in the village still were about the Donellans. 'Our Pierce', Sue had said, as if she were somehow related. It was no wonder Pierce had said that he sometimes felt as if he was living in a goldfish bowl, every move watched by outside observers.

'There's not a lot of point in fussing with your hair!' Sue exploded in exasperation. 'In this rain you'll look like a drowned rat two seconds after you set foot outside.

So what's she like? I'm dying to know,' she went on, frank curiosity in her voice. 'Gorgeous, I suppose? It'd have to be nothing but the best where the potential Mrs Pierce Donellan is concerned.'

'Mrs Pierce Donellan'. The words seemed to stab at Natalie, making her wince inwardly. 'Mrs Pierce Donellan'. Nearly ten years before, in the throes of her first, overwhelming adolescent crush, her fourteen-year-old self had whiled away long, lonely evenings doodling that name all over her notebook, enclosing it in hearts pierced by arrows. Like many a lovestruck innocent before her, she had allowed herself to dream that one day she might actually be able to have the title for herself. That was before her mother, stern reason, and finally Pierce himself, had firmly disillusioned her.

With an effort Natalie dragged herself back to the present, flashing Sue a swift, meaningless smile.

'I don't really know. But, like you said, she'll be absolutely gorgeous—Pierce's women always were—with the sort of style that just drips designer glamour—the type of thing that we poor nursery-school teachers could never dream of aspiring to.'

She turned another rueful glance on her reflection as she spoke, knowing that her private jealousy was showing through the cracks in her self-control. When compared with the string of beauties with tumbling blonde hair, patrician cheekbones and elegant height with whom Pierce, in his own words, had 'played the field', her own softly curved frame seemed positively ordinary. The darkness of her hair and eyes, together with a lush fullness to her mouth, had often led people to imagine the possibility of some exotic ancestry in her background, but the truth was that her family history was no more interesting than Sue's, whose mother, like her own, had come over from Ireland in search of work and had settled in the area.

'She'll make the perfect Lady of the Manor,' Sue put in. 'She has money of her own, an irreproachable background, and all the right connections.'

But she'd broken off the engagement. Natalie bit her lip hard to force back the impetuous comment that had almost escaped her. She had promised Pierce that she wouldn't tell anyone.

And the fact remained that Sue was right. Phillippa *had* had all the right qualifications to become the bride of the man known locally as the Lord of the Manor, while she—

She was what? Last night Pierce had called her a friend, but now, looking at the events of the night in the very much colder light of day, she was forced to wonder if even that had been honestly meant. Did *friends* behave as he had done?

And then, when she was quite unprepared to cope with it, her mind threw up the memory of the night of her eighteenth birthday, six years before. Then, buoyed up by the effects of the first bottle of wine she had ever drunk—wine that Pierce himself had provided in honour of the occasion—she had stumblingly tried to tell him how she felt, the emotions that filled her heart building up to a point where she had to let them out or explode from the strain of trying to hold them back.

Pierce had simply laughed.

'No, you don't, Nat,' he said, his tone indulgent as if humouring a wayward and none too intelligent child. 'You only think you do; you're far too young to know anything about such things.'

If he had slapped her hard in the face, he couldn't have shocked or hurt her more.

'I'm not too young!' she protested, her eyes almost black with pain. 'I'm eighteen—and that's quite old enough for what you really have in mind!'

The change in his face was shocking, the sapphire eyes narrowing until they were mere slits in his face, every muscle hardening, drawing his skin tight across the strong bones of his face until it seemed almost translucent, white marks of anger etched at the edges of his eyes, nose and mouth.

'And what, precisely, might that be?'

The bite of his cold, clipped words was as savage as the iciest wind from the North Pole, shocking Natalie into fearful silence, but when she would have simply shaken her head, unable to answer, he reached out and took her arm in a fiercely bruising grip.

'Tell me!' he insisted, his voice harsh and dangerous. 'I want to know.'

'You don't need me to tell you!' Natalie flung the words into his hard, set face. 'After all, everyone knows that there's only one thing a man like you wants from a girl like me!'

The last syllable fell into a silence so appallingly resonant that she felt it almost as a physical thing, closing around her, turning her blood to ice, stretching her nerves taut as she waited for Pierce to speak. When at last he did respond, it was with another laugh, but this time one that was so very far from the indulgent amusement of moments before that its harsh travesty of humour seemed to splinter the air around them.

'That's your mother speaking—I can hear her voice in every word. You're just parroting her clichés.'

'They're not clichés—she had experience—'

'Oh, *she* had experience, I grant you. But because some other employer tried it on with her, used her, abandoned her when she was pregnant, because some other rich man proved himself a louse, you've got me tarred with the same brush.'

The stem of the glass he held actually snapped under the pressure of his fingers and he tossed the two pieces onto the table as he got to his feet, pushing back his chair with an ugly, scraping sound.

'But believe me, little girl, that dreadful fate your mother is so convinced could be in store for you couldn't be further from the truth. For one thing, messing around with the likes of you could force me into a premature marriage—a prospect I don't view with any pleasure at all—and for another—'

He was turning towards the door as he spoke, but, unexpectedly, he paused on the threshold and swung back to face her, his eyes bleak as a winter sea.

'I think you ought to take the time to ask yourself one question—and that is if there's only ''one thing'' I ever wanted from you—' he laced the quotation with acid that burned agonisingly 'then why have I never so much as laid a hand on you in all the time I've known you? Why have I never done this—?'

And before she knew what was happening he was at her side, hard fingers closing bruisingly over her shoulders as he dragged her up out of her seat and close to his lean strength, his savage intent blazing in the brilliant blue gaze as his dark head came down swiftly, the cruel force of his mouth crushing her lips so violently that a whimper of pain escaped her. Pierce held her there just as long as he wanted and then, with a suddenness that jarred every bone in her body, released her again, sending her reeling back against the wall, her hand going out for support.

'If your mother had been right,' he flung at her in a dangerous undertone that was somehow a hundred times more frightening than any threatening shout, 'then *that's* what would have happened years ago—that and one hell of a lot more!'

And as Natalie still struggled for breath, her mind just a red haze of pain, he was gone, striding out into the darkness and the rain without so much as a backward glance, the sound of the door slamming shut behind him driving home the message that he would never, ever come back.

'Natalie?' Sue was concerned by her withdrawn abstraction, her voice jolting her back to the present, the stab of pain the memory brought pushing her into unguarded speech.

'Well, I just hope that any woman who's fool enough to say yes to our Pierce knows what she's taking on with him. I mean, he's a wonderful catch, our Lord of the Manor, but as a marriage prospect—*please*! After all, he's—what—thirty-three now, and never shown a sign of settling down. We've all heard the stories of his incredible sex life, seen the endless stream of women he's flaunted up at the Manor—'

Common sense told her that she'd said enough—too much in fact—but the pain deep inside was driving her on, pushing the rash words from her mouth.

'I doubt if he knows what the word faithful means. And you could never call Pierce Donellan a one-woman sort of man, could you? One woman a *month* is about his average—but one woman for *life*? I doubt if he could cope with the deprivation. I mean, just think of all those other girls out there in the big wide world, just waiting to fall into his bed if he'll just crook his little finger, flash them that smile, and—'

Suddenly it dawned on her that Sue's reaction was not one of simple interest or amusement.

'What is it?' she asked, frowning as she tried to interpret just what message the other woman was trying to telegraph with her wide eyes and expressive eyebrow movements.

'I think that's enough,' her friend hissed in a disturbed undertone. 'You'd better leave it there.'

'No, don't,' put in an all too familiar voice from somewhere behind her. 'I'd much prefer it if you carried on—I'm finding this character sketch most enlightening.'

'Pierce!'

Natalie didn't even have to look round to know exactly who had spoken. She knew every note in that deep voice, every shade, every nuance, and in the second before she spun round all colour fled from her cheeks, only to be replaced by a rush of burning heat as her stunned gaze collided with the coldly brilliant sapphire-blue eyes that were regarding her with sardonic amusement.

'Please do continue,' he invited in a dangerously soft drawl. 'I'm sure you haven't said all you wanted to; there must be so many other aspects of my personality you can do a demolition job on—why stop with my love life?'

'Pierce—'

It was all she could manage, shock making her dumb and numbing her brain so that she found it impossible to think.

'Where—where did you spring from?' she managed at last, her whirling imagination forming crazy thoughts of him appearing magically from nowhere, materialising in a puff of smoke like some pantomime demon king.

'I left the Porsche in the car park and came in through the main entrance.'

The deliberately pedantic response was an even clearer indication of his frame of mind than the disturbing edge to his voice, sending a shiver of apprehension down her spine.

'From there I was guided in the direction of the staffroom by the sound of your voice. 'It's amazing how clearly even a whisper will carry along silent corridors, especially in a building as old as this one.'

Which got the point across very nicely, Natalie reflected miserably. How much of her foolhardy speech *had* he overheard? And after last night just what was going through his mind?

'You—you should hear it when the children are in during the day,' she tried on a weak attempt at laughter, hoping, if not to appease him, then at least to turn his attention onto other, less dangerous topics. 'It's positively deafening then, isn't it, Sue?'

Her glance in the direction of her silent friend was touched with a desperate appeal for help which clearly puzzled the older woman even more than the obvious undercurrents she could sense in the scene before her but couldn't begin to understand.

'Aren't you going to introduce me to your friend?'

'Of course.'

The realisation that Pierce had caught that brief, betraying glance made something inside Natalie twist painfully as, shamefaced as a reproved child, she made a rather wild gesture in Sue's direction.

'This is Susan Hammond—she's the deputy head here,' she explained hastily. 'And of course you know Mr Donellan, by sight if nothing else, Sue. He—my mother used to work for his family up at the Manor.'

Which she hoped would satisfy the curiosity showing frankly in her friend's eyes. She had no idea why Pierce had turned up at the school like this—in fact, she was surprised that he even knew she worked here—but if she wasn't careful his unexpected visit would create the sort of gossip she had tried so very hard to avoid.

'Pleased to meet you, Mrs Hammond.'

Pierce took Sue's hand in a grip that Natalie knew from experience was warm and firm, but his smile she recognised as the polite one he used when he was obliged to make conversation with strangers or people who didn't particularly interest him. She had seen him use it often enough during formal occasions at the Manor or when faced with the major events in the village's social calendar. Hardly anyone saw the restraint behind it, but that was because only a carefully chosen few had ever been on the receiving end of the megawatt brilliance of the genuine, unrestrained warmth he could show when he wanted. Once upon a time she had been one of that select few, which was why, unhappily, she now knew she was no longer amongst their number.

'I hope you'll accept my belated congratulations on your engagement.'

Sue could have no idea of the way Natalie's heart lurched in painful response to her polite remark or the agonising tension that pulled at her nerves as she waited for Pierce's reaction, not daring to look into his face, fearful of what she'd see there.

'Thank you.' The smoothness of his tone had her catching her breath in shock. How could he remain so supremely calm, so totally in control when she was a quivering bag of nerves?

Because, of course, the question of his engagement or the breaking of it, and his subsequent all too brief involvement with herself—their one-night stand—she forced herself to admit the unpalatable truth—meant little if anything to him.

This, then, was how it was meant to be in the future, she acknowledged with a dreary sense of emptiness. Whether Pierce wanted any more to do with her or not, he had no intention of making their relationship public. They would always have to pretend, act as near-strangers in anyone else's company.

'But I'm sorry,' Sue continued. 'I should have asked why you're here. Is there something I can help with?'

'I don't think so, unless you know where Ray Donald is. We'd arranged to have a game of squash together tonight, but something's come up and I'm going to have to cancel.'

Natalie clamped her teeth down hard on her lower lip in order to bite back the cry of distress that almost escaped her as she struggled to come to terms with the possibility that she had been even more of a fool than she could have believed possible.

She had crept out of her own home—out of Pierce's bed—this morning in order to avoid embarrassing him or causing any emotional discomfort. Now she was forced to wonder whether Pierce would have felt any such thing in the first place. Certainly he showed no sign of it, simply turning up at the school as cool as you like—to talk about a game of squash!

Had she just been deceiving herself, then, thinking he would find it difficult to face her? Wasn't that just transferring her own feelings onto him? Wasn't the truth that Pierce, with his much greater experience in these matters, was quite used to handling them as if they meant nothing—which to him they probably did?

And that led to an even more painful consideration— the possibility that those emotive words 'I need a hand to hold' had been spoken with cynically deliberate calculation, that he had known exactly the effect they would have, their impact planned with callous precision.

'Oh, I'm afraid you've just missed him—he left for home five minutes ago.'

'Oh, well, perhaps I'll give him a ring later.'

He half turned towards the door but then he suddenly swung back again as if a new thought had crossed his mind.

'Perhaps I could give you a lift home, Natalie? After all, I have to pass Holme Road on my way out of town.'

'I usually catch the bus.'

That casual tone might deceive Sue, but she had enough experience of Pierce's moods to know that, like that social smile, it concealed a very different intent. She should have realised that the character assassination she had indulged in wouldn't be forgotten that easily, and the thought of the retribution Pierce might demand sent a second, more intense shiver of apprehension down her spine.

'In this weather? You'd drown before you reached the stop.'

Something in those blue eyes told her that he'd recognised her attempt to dodge his invitation and was equally determined not to let her get away with it.

'And you were just saying how difficult it would be to get those paintings home without them being ruined by the rain.'

Sue was fastening her briefcase as she spoke, and so didn't see the look of consternation that crossed Natalie's face at the way her friend's contribution had manoeuvred her into a position that left her with no alternative but to accept the offer of a lift. But Pierce had caught it, and his smile in response was a blend of triumph and mocking challenge that had her gritting her teeth against the furious words she longed to fling in his face.

'That would be very kind of you—if you're sure it's no bother.'

Her very politeness revealed precisely how she was feeling to anyone who knew her as well as Pierce did, but the satirical comment she had nerved herself for didn't come. Instead Pierce simply stooped to lift the box from the floor, tucking it securely under one arm.

'I'll carry this out to the car for you. Goodnight, Mrs Hammond.'

Which cut off any chance of escape, Natalie reflected ruefully, knowing she had no option but to follow him. It was either that or watch Class Three's precious artwork disappear without trace, and evidently Sue thought so too.

'A man who doesn't take no for an answer,' she murmured with a wry smile. 'You'd better get after him before he realises you haven't obeyed orders. I wouldn't like to see him when he's *really* angry.'

Natalie didn't need the implied warning; she was already reaching for her handbag.

'I'll see you tomorrow, Sue,' she flung over her shoulder as she hurried after Pierce, breaking into a run in an attempt to catch up with his long, forceful strides.

He had reached the main entrance before she came alongside him, clutching at his sleeve to force him to a halt when he would have marched out into the driving rain.

'Pierce—I'm not going *anywhere* with you.'

The look he turned on her was one of total disbelief, and she knew that he had understood the deeper subliminal implication of her words as well as their more obvious surface meaning.

'You'd rather trail home on the bus than travel in comfort with me?' His tone, like his expression, questioned her sanity.

'I—'

What could she say when already every nerve in her body was reacting, telling her how appalling a mistake it would be even to think of getting into the car with him? Seeing him so unexpectedly in the staffroom with Sue as unknowing chaperon was one thing, but being confined with him in the restricted space of the car, so close that she could smell the tang of his aftershave, hear his breathing, even sense the warmth of that lean, powerful body, was a very different matter entirely.

She had told herself that last night had been a moment out of time, that she shouldn't—couldn't expect anything more, and she had tried to accept that. What she hadn't anticipated was this total lack of any emotion, this complete wiping of the incident from his mind so that it was as if it had never happened, and she couldn't bear it any longer.

'Don't be bloody stupid, Nat!'

The use of that old, affectionate nickname almost destroyed her, breaking through the defences she had been trying to build round herself.

'It isn't stupid—I'm being realistic!'

Natalie was disturbed to find that her voice lacked the control she wanted, cracking awkwardly in the middle of the sentence, and revealing with embarrassing clarity the unsettled state of her emotions, but desperation gave her the words to drive home her point, not stopping to think how much she actually meant any of them.

'We both know how your family would react to their precious only son being seen with the daughter of their cook—her *illegitimate* daughter,' she added with bitter emphasis.

'You sound just like your mother now,' Pierce snapped, the coldness of his words as sharp as the lash of a whip.

'And you sound just like yours!'

'Is that so?'

Danger lurked in his voice, like broken glass at the bottom of a pool, and she gave a cry of shock as he dropped the box of paintings onto the floor, taking a step forward, his hands coming out and closing over her shoulders.

'What are you doing? Pierce?' she tried again as strong fingers probed the delicate bones at the tops of her arms, the nape of her neck, the effort to crush down her body's immediate response to his touch all but depriving her of the ability to speak.

'I can't feel it.'

'Feel what? Pierce—what are you talking about?'

'That really is one hell of a chip you've got on your shoulder.'

'And if I have, who put it there?'

'Oh, so now we're back on the old theme of there's only one thing he's after, right?'

'Right!' Natalie's tone matched his for cynicism. 'Except that you're no longer after it, are you? You got what you wanted last night, so there's no need for you to hang around.'

'Oh, isn't there? Natalie, look at me.'

Stubbornly she kept her face averted, the warning in that ominous use of her full name making her blood run cold in her veins.

'I said look at me, damn you!'

A rough hand came under her chin, forcing her head round so that her shadowed brown eyes had to meet the cold anger of his blue ones, the icy flame that burned there seeming to sear right to her heart.

'If you're determined to end this, Natalie, then I can't stop you,' Pierce flung at her harshly. 'But I think you ought to be damn sure you know what you're saying.'

'End it? There's nothing to end—you know that, I know it. And you need have no doubt that I know exactly what I'm saying—and I mean every word—so you had better believe it!'

She knew the moment that she'd succeeded in driving him away from her, seeing it in the way his expression changed, his face closing up, heavy lids hooding his eyes, shutting her out. She'd done it, she told herself miserably. She'd lost him for good now, had killed anything he might ever have felt for her by the force of her outburst.

'Right,' Pierce said, and the cold, clipped enunciation sounded the death-knell of the warmth they had shared so briefly in the night. 'I think you've made your point perfectly clear.'

She had done what she had set out to do, she told herself, her shoulders hunching against the terrible, dreary sense of inevitability that took possession of her as she watched him walk out into the rain, striding away from her without a single backward glance. She had driven him away from her, sent him out of her life for good. She would never see Pierce again except in the way that all the rest of the village saw him, as the Lord of the Manor, distant and aloof. And the pain of that loss would be like an incurable wound on her heart, always with her for the rest of her life.

CHAPTER FIVE

FIVE weeks later, Natalie knew that she could no longer escape from the fact that her one night with Pierce would be impossible to forget for very physical reasons as well as the emotional ones. No matter how much she tried to dodge the issue, the fact remained that she was putting up with some obvious symptoms that couldn't be ignored—something that didn't escape Sue's eagle eyes.

'You seem peaky,' she commented one morning when they met for a much needed coffee break. 'In fact, you're looking positively washed out.'

'I'm not feeling too brilliant,' Natalie admitted, concentrating fiercely on pouring boiling water into mugs. 'But then, we're all pretty much at the end of our tethers, what with the pantomime, the nativity play, parties—'

'Parents' evenings—I know,' Sue chimed in. 'But with you it looks more than that. Are you sure you haven't got this flu that's going around?'

Natalie sipped at her drink and immediately wished she hadn't. Just lately she had gone right off coffee; simply the smell of it was enough to turn her stomach.

'I'm going to spend the whole weekend in bed,' she added with a confidence that she hoped was convincing. 'If I do nothing but sleep, that should put me right.'

Not that she convinced herself, she was forced to admit. As she knew, much to the cost of her peace of mind, the comforting excuses of overwork or a dose of the flu no longer rang true in the light of the events of the past few mornings. She *had* been working hard, throwing herself into her job with an enthusiasm and dedication that was aimed at distracting her from any thought of what had passed between her and Pierce, and as a result had forgotten to check her calendar, count off days, and by the time she had thought to do so it was already too late.

Deep down, she had known it was too late on the first morning that she had woken with her stomach churning nauseously, dashing to the bathroom as soon as she set foot out of bed. Even then, she had allowed herself the comforting delusion of a possible twenty-four-hour bug. But when the twenty-four hours had turned into forty-eight, and then seventy-two, she had known she was on a losing wicket, and by the end of the week, when her symptoms, far from abating, had in fact grown worse, she'd known she couldn't fool herself any longer.

'Seen anything of our delectable Lord of the Manor lately?' Sue asked now, and the laughing nickname seemed to stab straight into Natalie's heart like a blade of ice.

Since she had returned home on that first evening, after the dreadful scene at the school, to find that every trace of Pierce's presence had been erased from her home, even the sheets he had slept in stripped from the bed and put into the washing machine, the programme timed—deliberately, she was sure—to finish just as she set foot over the threshold, she had known that she could be in no doubt as to just what message Pierce meant to convey.

The fact that he had left no answer to her note, not even a casual 'Thanks for the bed' scrawled at the bottom, only emphasised the distance he wanted to put between them. In fact, the slip of paper on which she had written to him had disappeared, and even though

she had carefully searched the kitchen in the hope that
he had left some form of communication there had been
no sign of it anywhere. There was no room for hope that
he might have called at the school looking for her, only
the dreary conviction that she had been right in con-
cluding that he wanted to act as if the night they had
shared had never been.

'Nothing at all,' she managed now in answer to Sue's
question.

'Neither has anyone else. Ever since the news broke
he seems to have disappeared off the face of the earth.'

'Well, that's hardly surprising, is it?'

For weeks the village had been buzzing with the story
of Pierce's broken engagement. It had certainly proved
more than the proverbial nine-day wonder.

'Oh, come on, Nat! You don't really think he's nursing
a broken heart, do you?' Sue laughed at her friend's
dubious expression. 'People like the Donellans don't
marry for the reasons we do. Love and other such paltry
considerations don't come into it at all. They get wed
for dynastic reasons, pure and simple, the combining of
exclusive blood, or, more likely, of extensive fortunes.'

'But Pierce...'

Pierce had come to her in the darkness of the night.
He had seemed distressed; certainly, he had behaved in
a way that was totally unlike the man she had known
before.

'You think he really loved her? Oh, well, of course
you know him better than any of us, so on that I'd have
to bow to your superior knowledge.'

Natalie managed a strangled response that Sue could
interpret in whatever way she wanted. The truth was that
she didn't really *know* Pierce at all. She had known him
for more than twelve years, but only from a distance;

she didn't know what he was really like—and she certainly hadn't recognised the man who had turned up at her home that night—the man who had made love to her—who had very probably made her pregnant.

And wasn't she fooling herself by believing that he had felt any of the emotions she had ascribed to him? Wasn't it more likely that, smarting from the way Phillippa had jilted him, he had looked for a way to salve his male pride? Any woman would have done, but she had been close at hand, and he'd known exactly which buttons to press in order to win her over.

'I think you'd better get home.' Sue was looking at her with some concern. 'You really don't look at all well. Go straight to bed, and don't come back until you're well and truly better. We don't want you infecting all the rest of us.'

'Don't come back until you're well and truly better.' The words replayed over and over in Natalie's head, gaining an added dark irony with each repetition, as she lurched out of bed the next morning, heading blindly for the bathroom once more. If she were to do as Sue had instructed, then she would have to stay off work for the next eight months—until some time in late July, if the frantic calculations that had kept her awake last night had been accurate.

There could be no doubt at all about what was 'wrong' with her now, and she managed a small, grim smile at the thought that her friend had no need to worry—this particular problem was not one that she could pass on as easily as Sue had feared.

'So this is why you've been avoiding me.'

The rough, harsh voice broke into the silence of the empty house with an abruptness that had her swinging round in shock, then immediately wishing she hadn't as the jerky movement worsened her discomfort, forcing her to hold onto the side of the washbasin for support, her legs feeling like cotton wool beneath her.

'Don't you think I had a right to know?'

To her blurred eyes, the intruder appeared as just a dark, ominously threatening shape in the bathroom doorway, seeming to her whirling thoughts to have appeared from nowhere like some fearful pantomime demon, lacking only the puff of smoke and the sound of a firecracker to make the effect complete.

'Well?' Pierce demanded savagely. 'Have you got anything to say or are you just going to try and pretend that this isn't happening?'

He took a single, angry step forward and the dangerous movement jolted Natalie into nervous speech.

'I haven't been *avoiding* you!' she gasped. 'It's not exactly easy to make contact with someone who isn't what you'd term *available*. You haven't been anywhere near Ellerby—'

'There are such things as phones.'

'So there are!' She didn't trouble to hide the bitterness in the words. 'Isn't that rather a case of the pot calling the kettle black?'

'And just what is that supposed to mean?'

'That people who live in glass houses shouldn't—'

'Natalie…' If his voice had been worrying before, now it was positively dangerous. 'Would you please stop parroting proverbs at me, and tell me exactly what you're talking about?'

'You surely don't want me to spell it out, do you?' Natalie flung at him, but then, overwhelmed by another spasm of sickness, she was forced to abandon the argument, once more leaning miserably over the basin.

'Oh, hell.'

Dimly she was aware of Pierce moving swiftly into the room, and the tap being turned on. A moment later, in a welcome pause from the appalling retching, he wrung out a flannel in the warm water and then wiped her face with it gently, smoothing the damp dark hair back from her forehead with his other hand.

It felt so good that for a moment Natalie allowed herself to forget who he was, and the part he had played in all this, and simply closed her eyes, leaning back against him and enjoying being cared for. But then reality struck home with a vengeance, and her eyes flew wide open again as she twisted round to face him.

'Go away!' she snapped, her dark gaze clashing with his watchful blue one.

'No,' Pierce returned with calm obduracy. 'You need me. You need *someone*,' he insisted, seeing the flare of rejection in her eyes. 'And I do have some stake in all this. Are you all right now?'

'If you mean am I going to be sick again,' Natalie managed as her breathing slowed, the dreadful feeling in her stomach calming, 'then no, I don't think so.'

But there was no way she could describe herself as all right. In fact, she doubted if she would ever be all right again.

'Then let's get you back into bed.'

'No!' Her protest came unthinkingly, and she was totally unprepared for the black fury in the look he turned on her.

'Just who the hell do you think I am?' he demanded ferociously. 'Some sort of appalling monster who would force myself on you while you're in this state?'

'I—no—'

'You can't stay here.' Pierce ignored her stumbling attempt at a response. 'In case you hadn't noticed, it's freezing, and that bit of a thing you're hardly wearing...'

The scathing look he gave her reminded Natalie only too plainly that the skimpy pink T-shirt-style nightdress she had on barely reached to her thighs, which meant that when he had first arrived and she had been bent over the basin...

Hot colour flooding her whole body, she suddenly saw her bed as a place of refuge. At least there she could pull the covers up to her chin, conceal what suddenly seemed like acres of exposed flesh.

'Steady,' Pierce advised as she blundered frantically towards her bedroom door, stumbling awkwardly in her haste. 'Now,' he went on when she was safely under the blankets and feeling just the tiniest bit more confident. 'Would you like a drink? Coffee?'

'Do you want me to be sick again?' Natalie demanded with a shudder. 'Because that's what'll happen if I so much as *smell* coffee. I could face some weak tea—and some dry toast is supposed to help.'

'OK, I'll be back in a minute—and then we have to talk.'

'We have to talk,' Natalie echoed in her mind as she huddled under the covers, listening to his footsteps descending the stairs. She couldn't help wondering just how many apocalyptic events had been preceded by those ominous words, and she wasn't at all sure that she wanted to hear what Pierce had to say.

'How did you get in here, anyway?'

She knew she was only delaying the inevitable, that there was no way she could possibly avoid the coming confrontation, but all the same she hoped that by going onto the attack like this she might at least earn herself a couple of minutes' reprieve in which to sip the tea Pierce had brought her and try to regain some much needed composure.

'I just walked in,' Pierce responded easily, setting the tray down on the bedside cabinet. 'You left the door unlocked—a bloody stupid thing to do.'

'I was very tired last night!' Natalie flashed at him, infuriated by his critical tone. 'I thought I'd checked—'

'Well, obviously you didn't.'

Pierce picked up his own tea and settled himself in a chair opposite, leaning back and resting one ankle on his knee as he regarded her steadily across the top of his mug.

'So now don't you think we ought to talk about just why you were so tired? Although, from the look of you, *tired* is a complete understatement. You look dreadful—like a half-drowned kitten.'

'Well, thanks for the compliment.'

Natalie concentrated fiercely on the piece of toast she had broken off, nibbling at an edge of it as she struggled to suppress the wave of sheer feminine embarrassment that heated her skin. She didn't have to look in a mirror to know she was a sight. After a couple of weeks of this sickness, she was only too well aware of the way that her face appeared pallid and drawn, her hair lank and lifeless. And the nightdress was elderly, well past its best, badly faded from much washing.

'I suppose Phillippa looks absolutely perfect first thing!'

Too late, she saw her mistake and wished her words back, Pierce's dark scowl worrying in her present vulnerable state.

'I haven't seen Phillippa for over four months,' he said in a voice that made her shiver in spite of the cosy covering of blankets, the cold flash of anger in his eyes making her wish she felt better able to cope.

She might have thought that, sitting down, Pierce would seem less imposing, or at least less threatening, but, strangely, she found that in fact it had quite the opposite effect. With those devastatingly clear blue eyes now exactly on a level with her own, there was no escaping his penetrating gaze, the searing intensity of the way it was fixed on her face.

With his long body in a soft cream Aran sweater and navy blue cord trousers, indolently relaxed, his dark head cushioned against the back of the chair, he should have appeared gentler, much more approachable, but, looking at him, Natalie couldn't prevent fanciful and disturbing images of the Spanish Inquisition or a Gestapo interrogator sliding worryingly into her mind.

'And besides, *you* have a reason for looking—and feeling—rotten. You're pregnant, aren't you?'

'After the sordid spectacle you've just witnessed, I'd be a fool to try to deny it,' Natalie muttered, not liking that 'looking rotten' one little bit. But her self-esteem was already at rock-bottom; it couldn't possibly sink any lower.

'So were you ever going to tell me?'

After his total silence of the past weeks, the last thing Natalie had expected was that cynical intonation, and it stung sharply, pushing her onto the attack in order to hide her pain.

'It takes a while for such things to make their presence felt! And if you were so concerned about possible embarrassing repercussions from that night, why didn't *you* contact me?'

'I tried to,' Pierce returned sharply. 'I rang God knows how many damn times, but either no one answered or the phone was off the hook.'

'You could have called—' Natalie growled, not wanting him to see how he had taken some of the wind out of her sails.

All those nights when she had been at school until late—at meetings, making costumes, rehearsing the play—had he been trying to contact her then? And later, when she had finally reached home, she had often been so completely worn out that she had unplugged the telephone and crawled into bed, often forgetting to plug it back in the next morning.

'A little difficult to drop by Ellerby on my way to and from Los Angeles—I've been in America for the past month,' Pierce explained, seeing her frown of confusion. 'I had to go straight there the day after...' He let his sentence trail off, obviously unable to think of a suitable description for what had happened on that night.

'After we had sex,' Natalie returned starkly, taking a sip of tea and then wishing that she hadn't as his frown made her throat close up tight in discomfort. Why should he object to her calling a spade a spade? After all, he surely wasn't claiming that *he* had been making love?

'There was a message waiting on the answering machine when I got to the Manor—a couple of major problems in a contract we'd just signed needed sorting out, and I had to fly over to the States straight away.'

'You could have told me this when you called at the school.' When he had been so concerned to tell his squash partner that he had been called away, but not her.

'Did you give me a chance? And you made it plain that you didn't want to see me again so there was no point.'

But he had tried to phone her long distance, Natalie reminded herself, the thought going partway towards soothing her painful feelings. However, the slight touch of comfort was completely erased by Pierce's next remark.

'And I sent you flowers.'

'Flowers!' Her voice rose high and sharp enough to splinter glass. 'Oh, yes, you sent flowers!'

They had arrived that very first day, delivered five minutes after she had arrived home, a huge, glorious bouquet that must have cost a fortune, and fastened to them had been a card that read simply, 'Thanks for the coffee.' The *coffee*! Reading that, she had been strongly tempted to dump the whole thing in the dustbin.

'Do you really think that a bunch of flowers—however big—is enough to compensate for the loss of—?'

Too late, she realised what she had been about to say, and broke off abruptly, but Pierce had heard, and he pounced on her faltering words like a hunting cat on its prey.

'The loss of...?' he echoed dangerously. 'Why the hell didn't you tell me you were a virgin?'

'Do you have to make it sound as if it's the crime of the century? There are one or two of us left, you know! Or, rather,' she amended hastily, 'there were. Positively prehistoric, I know, but not all of us have your opportunities...'

She was choking on the bitterness now, her pain a sour taste in her mouth, a burning sensation that she had lived with for nearly six weeks. She could forgive Pierce almost anything, except for the one thing that had preyed on her mind ever since that night, eating away at her like acid.

Because now it seemed that he had proved her mother right. All those years, she had fought Nora to defend his honour, insisting that her mother had it wrong. But now she had to face the possibility that Pierce *had* only been after one thing, and with each day that he had stayed away the pain of that suspicion had grown worse and worse, until she was no longer sure whether she loved him or hated him.

'Do you give all your conquests roses?'

'I don't think of them as *conquests*! And the flowers were just for the drink—and for being there—for listening. I had intended something much more valuable for—'

'For the gift of my body!'

The words dripped satire to hide the anguish that was like a red-hot stake in her heart. Now he wanted to *pay* her for the night they had spent together. If he had wanted to make her feel cheap and dirty, he couldn't have found a better way to do it.

'Oh, please don't concern yourself with that. After all, as I said, being a virgin at my advanced age is quite unbelievable, isn't it?'

If she could just brazen it out, then he might not guess what was behind the brittle mask which was all she could let him see.

'I mean—it had to happen some time, didn't it?' Her attempt at laughter drew no response from his hard, set face. 'I wouldn't want to go to my grave a dried-up, unfulfilled spinster.'

The change in his expression frightened her. He hadn't spoken a word since she had broken in on him, but the cold blaze of his eyes set in features that could have been carved from granite was infinitely more disturbing than if he had got to his feet and shouted at her in a savage rage.

'It had to happen some time, Pierce,' she repeated shakily.

'And that's what friends are for...' The black cynicism was unbearable, making her want to fold her arms around her body, to stop herself from shattering into tiny pieces. 'And now that it has happened?'

'Can't we just forget about it?'

She didn't really hold out much hope that he would agree, and wasn't in the least surprised when he shook his head with inimical ruthlessness.

Relentlessly he persisted with the matter in hand. 'Now that it has happened, and you are pregnant, there is no way we can forget anything. The obvious question is— what am I going to do about it?'

'You don't have to do anything!'

This was what she had been afraid of from the start— that Pierce would feel obliged to do something.

'I have a duty...'

A *duty*! Pain made Natalie desperate.

'How do you know it's yours?'

The silence that followed her outburst was terrifying, dangerous, seeming to be permeated with an ominous sense of threat that chilled her blood so that she shivered involuntarily. But then Pierce brushed aside her foolish words with as much contempt as if they had been an irritatingly buzzing fly.

'After your statement earlier, I'd be a fool to imagine anything else.' He paraphrased her own words with deliberate sardonic coldness. 'And, that being the case, I can see only one possible route open to us. We'll have to get married—'

'That's *not* the only possibility!'

She would have sworn that it was impossible for his expression to grow any darker, for the icy fury in his eyes to become colder, but she saw it happen, that clear blue freezing like an arctic sea.

'You weren't thinking of—' You wouldn't dare, his expression said. Not my child!

'No— Oh, no.' Even to defy him, she couldn't pretend the idea of abortion had ever crossed her mind. 'But I can't marry you.' Not like this; not when he felt forced into it.

'Why not?'

'Well, why should I?'

'You don't have to sound so damn enthusiastic about the idea!'

Once again the pot was well and truly calling the kettle black. Pierce's flat monotone could never have been described as even remotely enthusiastic, and as a marriage proposal his declaration had been light-years away from her dreams. But then, of course, those dreams had been just that—foolish fantasies that, if she were honest with herself, she had known could never be in reality.

With a terrible, searing sense of despair, Natalie recognised the bitter irony in her current situation. All those years she had dreamed of one day having Pierce propose marriage, and now here he was doing just that, but the circumstances made it only too plain that marriage was not what he wanted at all, and that turned the dream into a nightmare come true.

'You don't want to marry me!'

Pierce's shrug dismissed her protest as irrelevant.

'Why not? I was planning on getting married anyway—thirty-three seems a good age to settle down, and, as I said, I've always wanted children. And there's no one else in the running for the position.'

His casual indifference hurt far more than if he had rejected her violently, leaving her to cope by herself.

'You make it sound like some sort of job: Wanted, one wife, age twenty to twenty-five, must be capable of child-bearing—hours to suit...'

Her voice trailed off feebly in the face of his stony-featured blank stare.

'If that's the way you want to see it,' he declared in the flat monotone she had come to detest. 'Before we go any further, I think there's one thing we'd better get clear—you're not claiming to be in love with me?'

'In love...?'

If there was one thing guaranteed to ensure that she could never tell him how she really felt, then it was that cold-blooded question, the total lack of emotion in Pierce's voice, the distant, shuttered expression on his hard-boned face. Love him! Right now, she might as well try to give her heart to a marble statue—it couldn't possibly be any more cold and unresponsive.

'In love with you?' she managed again, and was thankful that at least *something* had come out, even though her words sounded so tight and brittle that she could almost imagine she might see them shatter on the carpet in front of her. 'What ever put that idea in your mind?'

Another of those coldly indifferent shrugs had her gritting her teeth against a scream.

'I thought it might make things a little easier.'

Easier for who? For Pierce, naturally, because if she was fool enough—in his eyes—to love him, then she would be so much more malleable, more easily swayed into doing what he wanted.

'You once told me that you loved me.'

For a second Natalie actually closed her eyes against the stab of distress. Why did he have to remind her of that moment of weakness now, when she was least able to cope?

'When I was eighteen?' She forced her eyes open again, making herself smile straight into his watchful face. She even managed a laugh. 'Oh, yes, I had a terrible schoolgirl crush on you then.'

'Only then?'

'Schoolgirl crushes are for schoolgirls, Pierce. We all grow up—up and out of our former silliness.'

Though, of course, she hadn't grown *out* of anything. Instead, her adolescent feelings had developed into something much deeper, a woman's love instead of a child's.

'So I'm sorry to disappoint you, but my answer to your proposal—if that was what it was—is an unqualified and non-negotiable *no*!'

Ruthlessly she squashed down the weak protest from her heart. Pierce didn't love her, or even want to marry her. He had only suggested the idea out of a sense of duty. She wasn't the woman he wanted. Phillippa had been his first choice, and so she could never be anything but very much second best.

'Why the hell not? I want my child, Natalie. I want to know it, love it, see it grow up—'

'*You* want—*you* want!' Natalie flung at him bitterly. 'Tell me, Pierce—what's in this for me?'

'A husband who would support you—you wouldn't need to work ever again—a home...'

No word of love, of any emotion, but then, what had she expected?

'I have a home! What if I want to stay here?'

Her wild gesture was a mistake, drawing that cold, blue-eyed gaze to the room they were in, and as Pierce looked around him, eyes narrowed assessingly, she saw the room through his eyes—the shabby carpet with some patches worn almost completely through, the battered, old-fashioned furniture, faded curtains and bedspread—

'You'd have my child *here*?'

His child—that was all that mattered.

'Oh, of course, the Donellan heir couldn't possibly be born in a two-up, two-down terrace house! Your mother would have a fit!'

'Don't put words into my mouth!' Pierce roared. 'And don't bring my mother into this!'

'Why not?' At least she had provoked some sort of reaction from him. Anything was better than that deadly indifference. 'Don't you think she'd have something to say about it? Have you considered how she'd feel if you brought me home as your bride? Her *cook's* daughter—father unknown—'

'You'd be the mother of my child—her grandchild.'

'A brood mare! I could be that here just as well. I wouldn't be the first single mother to bring up her child quite successfully on her own. I don't need you—I have all I want.'

'But I have something you don't,' Pierce put in on a note of cold reason that sounded warning bells through the whirling haze that filled her mind. 'I have money—more than I know what to do with—and at times like this money can be *very* useful.'

A cold, creeping fear slid down Natalie's spine, making all the tiny hairs on her skin lift in tingling apprehension.

'I earn a good salary...'

Something dangerous flickered in Pierce's blue eyes and instinctively she flinched, dreading what was to come.

'Enough to fight a protracted and very expensive custody battle?'

'You wouldn't!'

Natalie felt cold all over, a sensation of dread shivering along her spine. It was as if the fairy tale of the princess and the frog had been turned upside down, everything happening the opposite way round. Having kissed her prince, she had seen him turn into a hateful, dangerous monster.

He still *looked* the same; he was still the same devastatingly attractive man she had lost her heart to all those years before. But now it seemed that behind the familiar façade was someone she didn't recognise, someone she didn't know or understand—someone of whom she was suddenly coldly, terrifyingly afraid.

CHAPTER SIX

'You couldn't!'

'Don't tempt me.' It came lightly, almost casually, but with a dark undercurrent that told Natalie more surely than any ferocious declaration that Pierce meant what he said.

'You'd fight me for my child?'

Instinctively she curved her arms protectively around her body under the bedclothes and, looking into Pierce's taut face, saw the subtle change in his expression, the darkening of his eyes.

'*Our* child, Nat—I am the baby's father.'

'I know that!'

If only he knew that that was why she already loved the child so much—because it was his, part of the man to whom she had given her heart all those years ago, knowing with a terrible certainty that she would never get it back.

'But that doesn't mean that I want you as my *husband*! What use is a husband to me?' A husband who didn't love her, who only wanted to marry her out of a sense of duty.

'I can give you plenty—'

'Oh, I'm sure you can!' Bitterness made her words ragged and raw. 'I presume we're talking about money again.'

'No, not money.'

Bewilderingly, Pierce's attitude had changed completely, his voice deepening, becoming disturbingly soft and intense so that just hearing it heated the blood in her veins, making her shift uneasily in the bed.

'There are other things between a man and a woman,' he told her softly, leaning forward in his chair, blue eyes holding brown. 'Things that matter so much more...'

'Oh, how like a man to bring it down to that.' The effort she was making to reject that almost mesmeric spell he was weaving made her voice hard. 'It's just sex.'

'Oh, no, Natalie. It's not *just* sex; I'm talking about passion—the sort of passion that burns you up just to think of it. Passion so intense that it strikes sparks between people in the night—as it did with us.'

'What passion?' Natalie dragged her eyes away from his, concentrating fiercely on putting her mug back on the tray, praying he wouldn't know she was lying through her teeth. 'I don't recall it being anything to write home about.'

'Then your memory isn't anything like as good as mine.'

His voice had dropped even lower, becoming a husky whisper that sent shivers down her spine in the same moment that he eased himself out of his chair, coming to the side of the bed in one silent, graceful movement.

'But if you didn't find it as fulfilling as you might have done—to be honest you have to take some of the blame for what happened...'

The blue eyes lit up with a teasing warmth that had Natalie struggling with two conflicting reactions, feeling alternately blazing hot and then freezing cold, as if she was in the grip of some raging fever, her discomfort made even worse by the way he slid onto the side of the bed, leaning towards her as he took both her hands in his.

She had never thought that he might interpret her reaction in this way; that he might think her distress had
in some way been his fault. If only he knew the truth!

'But I can promise you that next time it will be so
very different.'

'Next time? *Next time?* What on earth makes you
think that there will *be* a next time?'

Pierce smiled almost gently at her indignant
expression.

'Oh, there will be,' he told her, total self-assurance in
every word. 'There can't help but be a next time where
we're concerned. You might as well ask the sun to stop
rising—'

'No!' Natalie tried to interrupt but he simply ignored
her.

'Look, Nat—you've been around in my life so long
that perhaps I'd taken you for granted; certainly until
that night I never guessed—'

He broke off, shaking his dark head as if in confusion. Privately, Natalie envied him his freedom to
move. She seemed incapable of any such thing, that
sapphire-blue gaze holding her transfixed, unable to stir
or look away.

'I didn't know you could affect me in that way.'

'I *affected* you so much that you didn't even bother
to contact me—'

'I told you about that! Damn it, Nat! I *tried* to get
in touch, which was more than most men would have
done after the way you slandered me to your friend—'

'That wasn't slander—' Natalie tried, but once again
he didn't listen.

'And reading that bloody note! "About last night…"'
he began, and it was a couple of seconds before Natalie's
bemused brain latched onto the fact that he was quoting

from the letter she had left for him nearly six weeks before. '"We both know it meant nothing—"'

'I didn't—' she gasped, meaning to say that she had never meant it to sound quite as harshly flippant as that. She had been trying to appear sophisticated, relaxed about the whole thing, so that he needn't have anything on his conscience, but as she heard the words now they sounded much more cold than careless.

'Yes, you did. Look, it's all here.'

Reaching into his pocket, he tugged out a folded piece of paper and thrust it at her.

'Take it!' he commanded harshly when Natalie could only stare, unable to believe that he had actually kept it, or to begin to wonder why he had done so. 'Read it—aloud!'

If she had felt awkward before, now she wished that the ground would open and swallow her up. A swift glance at the note had shocked her; she didn't recall writing this, and yet it was the letter she had left.

'Read it!'

'"We both know it meant nothing—less than that. It was a silly mistake—the result of some rather fraught emotions—so just forget about it. I certainly will."'

And then, as if that weren't bad enough, there was also the final line which she had added at the last minute.

'"PS. Help yourself to breakfast—no charge for anything!"'

Every trace of colour leached from Natalie's face, leaving her looking almost green at the appalling ambiguity of that 'for anything'.

But it seemed that an earlier line was the one that had Pierce's attention.

' "The result of some rather fraught emotions",' he repeated drily. 'That and a touch too much alcohol, of course. If only I hadn't had so much to drink...'

His words jagged painfully on Natalie's already rawly exposed nerves.

'Are you trying to say that I got you drunk? Or that *you* had to get drunk before you could even consider touching me?'

'Damn you, no, Natalie!' Pierce caught her flailing hands in a painful grip, shocking her out of her bitter rage. 'I said *no*! It wasn't like that, and you bloody well know it because you felt it too.'

'Felt it?' Mutinously she refused to show any understanding. 'Felt what?'

'Oh, Nat—the passion we shared that night. You felt it; I know you did. It burned you up—it went through both of us like a bush fire.'

'Not me,' she asserted, but he simply laughed at her feeble attempt at rebellion.

'Yes, *you*. Believe me, Nat, I know women. I know when a woman is aroused, when she wants me—and you wanted me every bit as much as I desired you. I could feel it between us as soon as we touched. It was like some sort of volcanic explosion, like nothing I've ever felt before, and it could be so again. Oh, yes, it could!' he added as she shook her head furiously.

The crushing grip on her hands gentled like his smile, his strong fingers releasing her, and he smoothed a softly caressing thumb over her taut palm.

'But this time I promise it will be so much better, sweetheart. This time I've had nothing at all to drink...'

'Pierce...' Natalie tried warningly as he edged closer on the bed.

But he didn't appear to have heard the discouraging note in her voice—probably because, in spite of herself, she hadn't been able to inject into it any real conviction.

'This time I'll show you what it can really be like—I promise. After all, if you're going to have to face the repercussions of making love by carrying my child, then the least I can do is to introduce you to the pleasures as well. Come on, Nat.' He laughed when she shook her head again, more frantically this time. 'Don't be frightened.'

'It isn't that.'

But how could she tell him what was really wrong? How could she admit that, having tasted it before, she knew that if he did as he promised—and she had no doubt that he would—if he once more opened the door to the magical world of the senses that she knew could come from physically loving him, then she would never be able to endure existing without it again? She had caught a glimpse of that world the first time they had made love and knew, without hope of redemption, that if she ever again experienced its delights she would never be able to resist Pierce at any time in the future.

'It's—'

'Shh, little Natalie...' His words whispered round her like a soft, warm breeze, weaving a gentle enchantment as he leaned forward to rest his forehead against hers, his lips on her cheek. 'Don't fight it, darling—let me show you...'

She would never be able to resist him in the future... Natalie's own thoughts came back at her like a reproach. Who was she trying to convince? She couldn't resist him *now*—particularly now, when those soft, enticing kisses were all it took to awake the primitive, fiercely demanding need deep inside her.

The weight of the covers was suddenly too much for her to bear, the heat that had built up underneath them making her move restlessly in a way that betrayed her feelings more clearly than words could ever have done. The sigh that almost escaped her was captured by his mouth instead, crushed back down her throat by the pressure of his lips on hers, the weight of his strong body pressing her down into the soft pillows at her back.

'Come with me, Nat,' he cajoled huskily, punctuating each word with another enticing kiss. 'Let me show you how it can be.'

And it was just as she had always known it would be. She had no strength to fight, no will to even think about it. And why should she? a little voice questioned inside her head. Why should she resist something that she wanted so much, something that seemed as right and inevitable as breathing itself?

Her whole body soft and pliant as wax, she let her mouth open to the pressure of his, meeting the intimate invasion of his tongue with her own, mutely inviting, encouraging, and she knew a heady thrill of delight as Pierce's arms tightened around her, the powerful pressure all the warning she needed of the change in his mood from gentle sensuality to urgent, burning need, her heart jerking violently as she heard his laughter.

'You see—it's happening again. It's there already—and we haven't even started yet.'

With a sudden twisting movement he lifted away the blankets that were covering her, replacing their weight and warmth with the power of his own body so that there was no sneaking chill to cool her heated blood, or bring any hint of second thoughts. And even if any such foolish concerns had slipped into her mind they wouldn't have stayed there long, but would have been swiftly driven away by the golden haze of pleasure that filled her head, leaving her incapable of thought, of anything but sheer, instinctive response to every touch and caress, every kiss that seemed to find the most sensitive pleasure spots on her body and rouse them to yearning, singing life.

She wanted to touch Pierce, wanted to feel the warm satin of his skin, the taut strength of muscle underneath her fingertips, needed to tangle her hands in the silky darkness of his hair, but when she tried to reach for him, to tug open the buttons on his shirt, he made a rough sound of protest deep in his throat.

'Oh, no, my angel—not this time.'

Her wandering hands were captured in a grip that, in spite of its seeming gentleness, was impossible to break, and pulled upwards, imprisoned on the pillows above her head.

'This time you keep these to yourself,' he told her in a voice that was already thick with passion, blue eyes burning down into her wide brown ones as he fastened one long hand around both of her wrists, freeing the other one to trail slowly, lingeringly down her hair, over her shoulder, down to the aching sensitivity of her breast, laughing with soft triumph as he heard the whimper of response she was unable to hold back.

'This time *I* do all the touching...'

That wandering hand moved even lower, sliding under the hem of the brief nightdress, tracing burningly erotic patterns over the soft skin of her thighs, stroking the curve of her hips.

'I give all the pleasure—all you do is take, Natalie. You take all I give you—and learn just how it can be...'

The words were heard only vaguely over the pounding of her heart, the heavy pulsing of her blood through her veins, which sounded like thunder inside her head. Her whole body seemed to be on fire, burning up under Pierce's touch, her breathing shallow and ragged, barely dragging enough air into her lungs.

The pink nightshirt was eased from her and discarded somewhere on the floor, Pierce's dark head lowering to the valley between her breasts, his mouth hot against her sensitised skin, the tip of his tongue etching a sensual path up one smooth curve to circle the hardening peak with tormentingly teasing slowness.

'Pierce!'

It was a choked sound in her throat, her body arching helplessly, needing to feel more than that, to know a deeper, sharper intimacy, and she heard once more his soft laughter, the warmth of his breath giving an added intensity to her delight, one that was almost unbearable as it feathered over nerves already roused almost to the point of pain.

'Pierce—please—'

'Gently, little one—gently.' She could feel Pierce's smile against her skin. 'We've a long way to go yet...'

A long way to go! Natalie felt as if her mind would shatter just to think of it. She couldn't take much more, couldn't wait any longer—

But at that moment Pierce's mouth captured one taut, expectant nipple and her thought processes stopped abruptly, her eyes wide open but seeing nothing, staring sightlessly at the ceiling. Her whole being centred on that one point of her body, on the sweet torment he was inflicting on it, the delight that radiated from it, like ripples flowing outwards from a stone thrown into a pool. She wanted to remain totally still, in order to concentrate all the more intently on that sensation, but found it impossible to do so, her body moving restlessly, her head tossing on the pillow, his name an incoherent litany on her lips.

It was only when Pierce shrugged himself free of his sweater that she was even aware of the fact that he no longer held her hands, that in reality he had released them long ago, using his fingers as well as his mouth to caress and tantalise, spark off sensations as sharp as an electric shock, as soft as the brush of a butterfly's wing. But still her arms stayed above her head, imprisoned there by some invisible force, the will to move them lost in the aching, spiralling hunger that seemed to reduce her body to one silent scream of need.

All she could see was Pierce. The only sound her ears could catch was his voice, murmuring erotic encouragement, impossible compliments. The warm, musky, intensely male scent that was so individually his seemed to enclose her in a heated cocoon, swirling round her like a mist, drugging her senses with each rawly indrawn breath. She could taste him on her lips, letting her tongue lap the salty dampness of his body like a small cat grooming its mate.

From feeling that she couldn't take much more of this delight without shattering into pieces, she had now come to wanting it never to stop, needing it to go on for ever and ever. Only that way could she hope to have enough. And Pierce seemed to understand her change in mood, intuitively responding, slowing his kisses, his caresses, making them sensuously subtle, infinitely gentle until her whole body was one blazing fire of sensation.

She could no longer keep her own hands still, risking his anger as she ran her fingers down the tightly muscled back, stopping at the leather belt that encircled the narrow waist and tracing it round to the buckle, tugging at it impatiently.

'Nat...' Her name was a note of warning.

'I want to touch you!' she protested. 'Want to feel you.'

'Oh, you will,' he promised thickly. 'You will.'

Sensing as intuitively as before just what it was she needed, he rolled onto his side for a moment, holding her still with the deep, demanding kisses that bruised her mouth, and when he came back to her he was as naked as she was, the heat of his skin searing hers as he crushed her to him.

'Can you feel me now, sweetheart—can you feel how I want you?'

Natalie could only manage a wordless murmur—one that fractured into a cry of delight as his fingers moved down over her stomach to the heart of her femininity, his touch bringing with it such an electric pulse of sensation that her body bucked and twisted beneath him. And the next moment those same hands that had caressed her so gently fastened around her hips in a clasp of steel, holding her tightly, lifting her to meet the thrust of his final possession.

'Now you can really feel me,' he muttered in her ear. 'Really know what it's like...'

He moved inside her, slowly at first, waiting, watching all the time for her to respond, to show her pleasure. But within only a very few seconds all Natalie's control had gone, and she knew nothing but the hunger he had awoken in her, the need at the core of her being all she could focus on, burning her up, taking her higher— higher—the savage rhythm building strongly, inevitably, to a crescendo of delight that had her crying aloud and clinging to his powerful body as if it was all that still held her anchored to the world.

A long time later her breathing slowed and she gradually drifted back to awareness, shaken by the reality of the delight she had known, beside which all the dreams, the imaginings were as nothing, light-years away from the ecstasy of the truth. It had blown her world apart, shattering it into a million splinters, and now that those tiny pieces had come back together again the image they showed was nothing like the way it had been before. Knowing what she did now, she could never, ever hope to be the same again.

Beside her, Pierce stirred lazily, sighing deeply as he stretched his long limbs in a movement redolent of sensual contentment.

'So now,' he murmured, his voice rich with dark satisfaction, 'you see what it should be like. And don't try to claim that you felt nothing that time, because it'll be a lie, and you know it as well as I do. I saw your reaction, felt your response—I *know*.'

He knew too damn much, Natalie thought on a wave of bitterness. Too much, and yet not quite enough—something for which she supposed she ought to be deeply grateful. Pierce knew how to make her body respond, how to make it sing like some beautifully crafted musical instrument, perfectly tuned to the touch of a maestro, but he didn't know—couldn't know—that the rest of her was his too. Her heart and mind, even her innermost soul, were his now and for ever, but he must never even begin to guess at that truth, because, for all the blazing passion he had shown her, she was not the woman he had chosen. She could only ever be second best, and when she heard his next words she knew that that fact alone was what must colour her response to them.

'So now tell me you won't marry me—if you dare. We've always been able to get along, Nat, and now we find we're unexpectedly good together in bed. Arranged marriages have been made to work from far less auspicious beginnings.'

But an arranged marriage, while it might suit Pierce's dynastic yearnings, would never be good enough for her. All or nothing, she had said, and she had meant it.

'No, Pierce—' she began, but he wouldn't let her finish.

'Remember, you wouldn't be marrying just for your sake, but for the baby too.'

The words were soft but with an inflexible edge that warned her he was never going to let the argument drop.

'Do you really want to bring your child up on your own, the way your mother did with you? Do you want to repeat her mistakes, letting it grow up without a father, always with that gap in its life—the missing piece of the jigsaw?'

The way Pierce quoted her own phrase back at her told Natalie that he knew exactly what he was doing. Hastily she bit down hard on her lower lip in order to suppress the cry of distress that almost escaped her, burying her face in the pillow so that he couldn't see her expression and know that his words had hit home. This was the one weapon that she had prayed Pierce would never use against her, the strongest force in his armoury, the one against which she had no possible defence.

'Think how it will be in the future. Ellerby is such a small place, a hotbed of scandal. Can you face all the gossip, all the prying, the talk behind your back—like mother, like daughter? Could you let your child face it? If you marry me, there'll be no talk—at least not after the first excitement has died down—and you'll have everything you need—everything you ever dreamed of.'

He ran a soft fingertip down the line of her naked back, making her shiver in involuntary response, her pulse quickening immediately.

'Think of it, Nat,' he cajoled. 'You'll have money, comfort—but above all else you'll have peace of mind and security—with respectability assured. Your baby— *our* child—will grow up in a proper home with two parents who love and care for it. Every child ought to have that sort of start in life, Natalie. If anyone knows that, you do.'

Oh, God, he had her cornered, trapped with her back squarely against the wall. She could bring out no argument to counter the one he'd used, and Pierce knew it. He of all people knew just how badly she had suffered from never knowing who her father was. Hadn't she always vowed that no child of hers would ever grow up with that same emptiness? And in an unguarded moment she had confided those same feelings to Pierce, unknowingly handing him the weapon that he was now using with such determined ruthlessness against her.

'This isn't fair.'

'No, it isn't,' Pierce acknowledged, his voice harsh. 'But to be perfectly honest I don't exactly feel like playing fair over this. That's my child you're carrying, and I have no intention of being an absentee father—'

'But you don't want me as well!'

Still Natalie couldn't bring herself to look at him, her protest muffled by the pillow.

'I'll willingly admit that this isn't how I would have wanted things to happen, but we have to play the game according to the cards fate has dealt us. Your pregnancy is a fact—it isn't up for debate—and, as far as I'm concerned, neither is the subject of marriage.'

A long, powerful hand closed over Natalie's shoulder, pulling her inexorably up from the pillow and turning her to face him. Looking up into his eyes, seeing how they seemed to have darkened to the navy blue of an evening sky, Natalie knew that she stood no chance against the ruthless determination that burned like a cold flame in their depths. The same unrelenting certainty was stamped forcefully into every tight muscle, etched along every powerful bone of his hard-featured face.

'Don't fight me on this, Natalie, because you'll only end up hurt if you do. You have no hope of winning, and I have no intention of ever giving in.'

'I—'

But even in the second that she opened her mouth to try to defy him again Natalie knew she was lost. All the strength to resist ebbed from her body like air escaping from a punctured balloon, leaving her limp and dejected.

After all, she couldn't avoid asking herself, why *was* she fighting him? And what was she fighting for? She loved Pierce, didn't she? She loved him and she was carrying his child, and because of that he wanted to marry her. It might only be second best, but it was something—all she was ever going to be offered—and, fool that she was, she was weak enough to settle for that.

And what had happened to all or nothing? Well, what Pierce was offering her was a long way from everything she had ever wanted, but it wasn't exactly nothing—nothing was what she would be left with if she refused him now. And if she accepted, then, as Pierce himself had said, arranged marriages started with less. Perhaps, one day...

No. To think like that was worse than foolish; it risked the pain of dreams that could never come true, the hope of a pot of gold at the rainbow's end that only existed in fairy stories. She had to do as Pierce had said—accept the hand that fate had dealt her, and play the game with that. To wish for any more would only lead to eventual despair.

'Natalie?' Pierce's voice was as hard and unyielding as his expression, his use of her full name a warning she knew she would do well to heed. 'I want an answer— what's it to be?'

Natalie drew in a deep, uneven breath, exerting every ounce of self-control she possessed in order to school her face and voice, knowing that how she answered would decide her future life for many years to come.

'All right,' she said, the words falling flatly from lips that suddenly seemed to be made of wood, no trace of emotion in the stiff response. 'For those reasons, then, I accept your proposal. For the baby's sake, yes, I will marry you.'

CHAPTER SEVEN

'GOOD evening, Mrs Donellan. It's bitter out, isn't it? You must be glad to be home. I've lit a fire in the sitting room, so it will be really cosy in there.'

'Thank you, May—I'll appreciate that.'

If there was one thing that brought home to her just how her life had changed in a few short weeks, Natalie reflected as she surrendered her coat and hurried into the firelit room, it was this, the regular evening routine.

In the past, after work she would have gone home to a cold, dark house, the silence seeming to echo round her as, usually still wearing her coat, she struggled to get some heat out of the old-fashioned solid-fuel boiler before starting on the preparation of a quick, simple meal. But these days she was picked up at the school gates in the chauffeur-driven car Pierce had insisted on putting at her disposal, knowing she didn't drive herself, and transported to the haven of warmth and light that was the Manor.

Here, she was greeted by the housekeeper—her mother's replacement—who had already prepared a tray of tea and sandwiches to tide her over until the time that Pierce came home, when a delicious, beautifully prepared dinner would be served in the elegant dining room.

The contrast with her previous way of life couldn't be greater, Natalie acknowledged, pouring herself a much needed cup of tea and sinking back into one of the huge chintz-covered armchairs, kicking off her shoes with a sigh of relief. But the trouble was that she couldn't ap-

preciate it properly. It simply made her feel more ill at
ease than ever. It wasn't for her, it was for that alien
creature, Mrs Pierce Donellan, wife of the lord of Ellerby
Manor.

But *she* was Mrs Pierce Donellan, even if she found
it impossible to believe. She didn't seem to have been
able to draw breath for a moment since Pierce's proposal—though ultimatum was a more accurate description. Since then she felt as if she had been lifted off
her feet by a whirling tornado, flung high in the air and
dropped down to earth again to find that nothing was
the same.

'But does it have to be so soon?' she had protested
when, the day after she had agreed to marry him, Pierce
had announced that the wedding would be in a week's
time, just ten days before the end of the Christmas term.

'I can see no point in delaying.'

His arrogant dismissal of her concern had been further
evidence—if she had needed any—of how little she actually figured in his plans. He wanted his child, and the
way to ensure he got what he wanted was by staking a
legal claim to it and marrying the baby's mother as soon
as possible.

'The sooner this is official the better as far as I'm
concerned.'

'But I haven't—'

'Everything's arranged—all you have to worry about
is finding something to wear and turning up at the church
on time.'

'The church! I would have thought that the regis-
try—'

'Well, you thought wrong. Donellans have been
married at St Oswald's for the past two hundred years,
and I don't intend to break with tradition this time.'

'But if the ceremony's at the parish church, then everyone will know—the whole village.' Natalie couldn't believe he would want anything so public. And St Oswald's was where he would have married Phillippa.

'Of course they'll know—that is the whole point. Natalie, we are getting married—you will be my wife. I don't intend hiding you away like some madwoman in the attic.'

'But this isn't exactly a normal marriage! After all, it's hardly a love match.'

'But we're the only ones who know that,' Pierce retorted, stunning her.

'We're— But your mother—surely she knows?'

'She knows just what I've told her.'

'And that is?'

'That I asked you to marry me and you accepted.' It was a flat, emotionless statement.

'But—haven't you told her *why* you asked me?'

'Of course not!' Pierce snapped, suddenly getting to his feet in a swift, restless movement. 'Do you want her to think that you've trapped me? That I've been forced into marrying you?'

Natalie wished he had remained seated. Towering over her like this, he seemed to dominate the small room, too tall, too powerful, too *male* to be confined in the suddenly tiny space. She didn't know him, she thought desperately, couldn't find any point of contact with this man she had promised to marry.

'But that's just what I have done! Be honest, Pierce— would you be marrying me if I wasn't pregnant?'

Pierce's dark face closed up, and he swung away from her without answering. But he hadn't needed to say a word; she could supply the necessary details herself. It was obvious, wasn't it? There was no way Pierce would even have considered marrying someone like her if she hadn't been carrying his child—the Donellan heir.

'You didn't force me.'

His voice was low and intent as he stared out of the window, but then suddenly he spun round to face her, his face set into harsh, taut lines.

'If anything, I trapped myself. It takes two to make a baby, and I knew exactly what I was doing when I made love to you that night. I wasn't that drunk, damn it!'

Natalie wasn't aware of her own expression having changed, but Pierce's sudden dark scowl told her that it had.

'But I should have been more careful. I want you to know that I'm not usually fool enough to have unprotected sex with just anyone—'

'Not usually.'

She couldn't keep the sarcastic words back, but at least they weren't as acidly bitter as the ones that burned in her mind, eating at her heart. 'Just anyone'—Pierce certainly knew how to make her feel small.

'You're not claiming you had no part in it, surely?' A muscle jerked in Pierce's jaw, revealing the struggle he was having to control his temper. 'You must know I never really expected that you'd actually get into my bed.'

'But you couldn't resist trying it on—'

'Don't be bloody stupid, Nat! No man with red blood in his veins would have been able to resist you in that incredible slip of a thing you called a nightdress.' Pierce's voice had softened noticeably, becoming low and slightly husky. 'You were all warm and soft from your bath and I wanted you like hell. But from the moment that I realised you were a virgin I should have thought—'

His sudden silence tightened Natalie's nerves, and with a fatalistic sense of inevitability she knew what was coming. She wasn't mistaken.

'Why were you still so innocent? I thought no one waited for marriage these days.'

'Perhaps no one asked me.' Striving for flippancy, she only succeeded in sounding coldly brittle.

'You can't expect me to believe that. For one thing, you told me about Gerry.'

'He was just a *friend*.'

Too late, she saw the trap yawning at her feet and couldn't avoid it. Pierce, of course, wasn't slow to pick up on it too.

'I thought that was all you said I was to you, and yet—'

But Natalie couldn't take any more. The ice was too thin beneath her; an unwary move and it would shatter.

'Are you trying to get me to say that in some weak, romantic little part of my heart I was really saving myself for *you*?'

She didn't dare to look into his face, for fear he would read the truth that she was sure must be etched onto her forehead in letters of fire.

'I'm not fool enough to assume that!' Pierce's laughter was cynical, grating on her rawly exposed nerves. 'But you have to admit that your behaviour isn't typical of today's liberated woman.'

'Well, for one thing, I was so busy with my studies. Mum had made so many sacrifices to get me to college, I wanted to do really well. And I never found the right man—I always wanted the first time to be really special—to mean something . . .'

The words died on her lips, shrivelled by the sudden blaze in those blue eyes.

'I'm sorry.' Just three clipped syllables, as cold and hard as his expression, but something about them pushed her into unguarded speech.

'Oh, don't be!' This time she managed the light-hearted carelessness rather better. 'Like you said, it takes two, and I—wasn't exactly unwilling. And in the end I was mistaken—it was nothing to make a fuss about.'

But Pierce's expression didn't lighten in response, remaining as dark and glowering as before so that she rushed on hastily.

'I only meant that I wish I hadn't waited so long.'

Oh, why couldn't she just shut up? She made matters worse each time she opened her mouth.

'After all, if I'd been less naïve you wouldn't be in this mess. I'm sure you'd prefer it to be otherwise—'

'Oh, I would.' Pierce's voice was low and husky, his eyes burning into hers as he spoke. 'You can't know how much I wish certain things had never happened. But they have, and all we can do is make the best of it.'

'Why are you sitting in the dark?'

Pierce's voice and the sudden snapping on of the light jolted Natalie back to the present, and she realised with a sense of shock that while she had been lost in her memories time had slipped away, the tea growing cold in her cup. And now Pierce was home unexpectedly early, well before she was ready to face him.

'I was thinking.'

'Of nothing too pleasant from the look on your face.' His tone jarred uncomfortably. 'And you've let the fire get close to dying—no wonder Mrs Newton was concerned.'

'I just wanted some time on my own. And besides—' she had to raise her voice above the rattle of the poker as he tended to the fire '—I don't like the thought of you getting the housekeeper to spy on me.'

That stopped him dead, his dark head swinging round to face her, blue eyes disturbingly distant.

'*Spying?*' he echoed with a coldness that made her wince. 'Isn't that something of an exaggeration? I merely said that—'

'I didn't mean it the way it sounded!' In the face of that cold-eyed scrutiny, all the fight went out of her like air from a pricked balloon. 'It's just I'm not used to this sort of life yet.'

And she wasn't used to this Pierce either. This man in the sleekly tailored business suit only aggravated her feeling of alienation and isolation. The elegant grey suit, white shirt and silk tie he had worn to travel to London transformed him into the Donellan of Donellan Software, very much the formidable businessman and very definitely the Lord of the Manor.

He had looked just this way on their wedding day too, a distant, withdrawn stranger, not the old Pierce, the one she would willingly have promised to love and honour for the rest of her days. This man was a very different prospect. She had no idea at all how she felt about him.

'And you caught me unawares. I didn't expect you back until much later.'

'You needn't sound so pleased about it.' The poker was slammed into its stand with a force that had her flinching back in her chair. 'Most newly married brides would be glad to think that their husband wanted to leave his business to fend for itself and hurry home to be with her.'

If she could believe that was true, how different life would be!

'But then, most brides would have had a proper marriage, and as they probably would have still been on honeymoon—their husband wouldn't have taken himself off to London in the first place.'

'You could have had a honeymoon.' Pierce's words were punctuated by the thud of pieces of coal as he built up the fire. 'You only had to say.'

'I know.'

Natalie's voice was low as she recalled the way she'd felt when he had offered to take her away after their wedding. Anywhere in the world, he'd said, for as long as she wanted. Wasn't there somewhere she'd always dreamed of visiting?

'But I'm not that much of a hypocrite.'

'Hypocrisy...' Pierce's tone was dangerous and Natalie could only be grateful that his attention was still on the fire. 'Is that how you see it?'

'Well, it would be, wouldn't it?'

With a sinking heart, Natalie realised that the conversation had once more fallen into the unhappy pattern that had become the norm ever since their sham of a marriage. It seemed that almost as soon as she had agreed to marry him Pierce had become a totally different person, one she neither knew nor understood. He had become distant and unapproachable, throwing himself into his work with an intensity that took him away from home for days at a time, and when he was at the Manor he kept communication between them to the absolute minimum necessary to keep up appearances.

Even the searing passion that had flared between them now appeared to have been like some wildfire, the result of a spectacular lightning strike that had blazed fiercely but briefly, burning itself out and then dying, leaving nothing but cold ashes in an empty grate. Since her arrival at the Manor as Pierce's wife she had slept in a separate bedroom, and never once, in the past ten days, had he even hinted that he wanted to share a bed with her.

'After all, a honeymoon is hardly appropriate to this sham of a marriage, is it? It would be just another lie—'

'A *lie*!'

She had overstepped the mark with a vengeance, she knew, as he took three swift strides towards her, strong hands closing over her upper arms and hauling her out of her chair, bringing her hard up against the elegantly suited length of his strong body.

'A lie, is it?'

'Pierce—'

'A sham?' Ruthlessly he ignored her shaky interjection, the dangerous glitter in his eyes closing her throat over any further attempt at protest. 'And what the hell do you think—?'

But then abruptly his mood appeared to change.

'A *lie*,' he repeated, but in a very different tone. 'Oh, yes, my sweet Natalie, our marriage is certainly a lie—but perhaps not in the way you think.'

'I—don't know what you mean.'

'No?'

The question came softly, huskily, and those blue eyes were as deep as bottomless pits, their expression unreadable as his mouth curved into a strangely gentle smile.

'Then shall I show you? Shall I show you just what a sham this relationship is?'

One hand slid under her chin, strong fingers lifting her face towards his.

'Take this, for instance...'

Warm lips brushed her forehead with unbelievable softness, the delicate caress sparking off a tingling response in every nerve.

'Or this...'

This time the kiss touched each eyelid in turn, pressing them closed, and she kept them shut, fearful of the emotions she felt sure must show if he looked into her eyes.

'Are these a sham, my lovely? Is *this* a lie?'

The mouth that captured hers was suddenly fierce, demanding a response that Natalie was incapable of holding back. Her own lips softened under his, opening to the invasion of his tongue, and she knew that her legs were weakening beneath her, the strength of Pierce's grip being all that held her upright as she sagged against him.

'How do you know what the truth is? I know only one thing that's real—one thing that's there between us that even you can't deny. *This* is no sham, my darling.'

Powerful hands swept over her body, crushing her up against him so that she couldn't be unaware of the physical evidence of the raw need that roughened his tone and made his breathing harsh.

'Pierce—' she tried again, but once more he ignored her.

'This is no lie—and neither is this—'

Once more his lips crushed hers in the same instant that one of those searching hands closed possessively over the soft swell of her breast, a moan of response escaping her as a fire of need flared inside, seeming to melt her bones in its heat.

'This is what's really between us, darling—it's why we're together, why we're married. I wanted you here so that I could do this—' another kiss, more demanding, more arousing than the first '—and this—whenever I wanted.'

Natalie's head was swimming, her chest heaving as she tried to breathe; the aching yearning that had uncoiled inside her was growing, spiralling out of control. She was incapable of anything beyond simply responding to Pierce's kiss, responding and trying to communicate her own desire, the passion that was rising to meet his.

The discreet tap at the door was almost inaudible through the pounding of her blood, the heavy beat of her raised pulse like thunder inside her skull, and even when it was followed by a careful cough she still wasn't able to drag herself back to reality enough to think or behave rationally.

Pierce, however, had no such problems. His head came up instantly, and the passion that had seemed to have him completely in its grip only seconds before vanished in an instant, hidden under the polite social smile that was switched on as if at the press of a button. His arm came around Natalie's waist, holding her still when she would have moved away from his side as he turned with relaxed composure to face the woman standing in the doorway.

'Yes, Mrs Newton?'

'I'm—sorry to disturb you, sir...'

The housekeeper sounded almost as embarrassed as she felt, Natalie thought shakily, hot colour rising in her cheeks at the thought of the passionate embrace, the intimate caresses that the other woman must have witnessed.

'Not at all.'

Natalie couldn't believe the ease of Pierce's response. He was apparently totally indifferent to the tangle of black hair that had fallen over his forehead, the smudge of lipstick on his mouth.

'Was that call for me?'

'It's Mrs Donellan—your mother—she's holding.'

'I'm coming.'

To Natalie's complete consternation, Pierce turned to her, resting his hand very lightly against her cheek before dropping a soft, almost playful kiss onto the tip of her nose.

'I'll be as quick as I can, sweetheart,' he murmured, leaving her gaping in confusion as he strode from the room.

Left alone, Natalie struggled with a bewildering tangle of feelings, not knowing which one was uppermost in her mind. The storm of passion that Pierce's kisses had awoken in her still left every nerve-end burning, each tiny cell tingling with heightened awareness and unappeased hunger, but added to the whirlwind of sensation was another, more devastating sense of loss that seemed to hold her heart in a coldly crushing grip.

'Was that call for me?'

Recalling Pierce's words, she realised—too late—that she had vaguely heard the telephone ring, but, carried away on a heated tide of sexual excitement, hadn't registered quite what it was. Not so Pierce, of course.

The stab of disappointment and bitter realisation was almost unbearable as she acknowledged that not only had Pierce heard the phone but, far from being rocked off balance as completely as she had been, he had been thinking coldly and clearly enough to realise that once the housekeeper had answered it then, knowing he was at home, she would inevitably come to find him with a message.

He had also been well aware of the fact that the door was ajar. His lack of surprise, the ease of his reaction made that only too plain—which led to only one disturbing and very painful conclusion. The display of uncontrollable passion, the heady kisses, the arousing caresses, even Pierce's whispered words, had all been just a display, planned for Mrs Newton's benefit.

But why? She was still trying to find a possible answer to that problem when Pierce came back into the room.

'I've been thinking,' he announced in yet another of those lightning-swift changes of mood that left her feeling as if she was on a merry-go-round whirling out of control. 'One of the ways to solve the problem of the time I have to spend away is for you to come with me.'

'To London?'

Absorbed with other, much more important concerns, Natalie found that the inane question slipped off her tongue while the one that was fretting in her mind stuck in her throat, refusing to be spoken.

'Of course to London—we could use a trip to make up for the missing honeymoon. Have you ever been before?'

'Once—for a day; it was a school trip to the National Gallery but I much preferred the Portrait Gallery. I went in there when everyone else was eating their packed lunches, and I could have stayed for hours, just studying faces.'

'I know what you mean. It's one of my favourite places—I often go there when I'm in London. Somehow seeing the portraits of real people makes history come alive in a way that books and facts can't.'

The choking sensation in Natalie's throat worsened as she saw Pierce's face change yet again, his smiling enthusiasm making him once more the man she had glimpsed so briefly in her youth, just after her accident—the intelligent, witty visitor who had shared her love of books and fascination with the past, and whose conversation had always been so absorbing that the time he spent with her had simply flown by.

But that time had just been a brief idyll of delight, over too soon. Her injured ankle hadn't even mended before he had gone back to London, turning his attention once more to his work and the more sophisticated company he found in the capital.

'I've always been intrigued by the might-have-beens—the people who would have been king if they hadn't died young. Henry the Eighth had an older brother, Arthur, who was originally married to Catherine of Aragon before Henry himself, and Charles the First was a second son too. I used to look at their faces and ask myself if things would have been very different if they had lived.'

'Would there ever have been an Elizabeth the First, you mean—or the Civil War? It's quite a thought. I'm afraid my own reactions weren't quite so deep.' Natalie's smile was slightly shamefaced. 'I completely lost my heart to Prince Rupert of the Rhine— I was only fifteen . . .'

'And he was quite a looker if I remember rightly.'

To her intense relief, Pierce showed no inclination towards the teasing questions she had feared. If he had probed any further, she might have let slip the fact that she had been so entranced by the Cavalier Prince because his darkly handsome features had reminded her irresistibly of the man who had stolen her adolescent affections—Pierce himself.

'He was another second son, too—though his brother lived to a good age—so Rupert was free to choose his own way in life, unlike the others who had their duty forced onto them.' Pierce turned to her, his expression sombre, his sapphire eyes dark and strangely thoughtful. 'I had an older brother, you know.'

'No, I didn't. You said *had*, Pierce—what happened?'

'He died—Oh, no.' He had caught her murmur of distress. 'He was only six weeks old at the time, so I never knew him, but it had repercussions for me.'

'In what way?'

'Well, naturally it meant that I was the one who inherited the role of Lord of the Manor.'

A role he didn't relish, his tone said only too clearly, making Natalie recall the withdrawal she had seen in him on occasions, his use of that polite, social smile.

'Is that why you wanted to start the computer company—so that, like Prince Rupert, you had some aspect of your life that was your own choice?'

'It had a lot to do with it. Even though my family was wealthy enough to support me in a great deal of comfort without my having to earn my own living, I wanted to make something of my own. And my father made sure I was well aware of the fact that wealth and position brought responsibilities as well as privileges.'

He'd used that word responsibility before, when she'd asked him why he'd wanted to marry, Natalie recalled, knowing a sharp twist of distress at the thought that his father's words must have been very much in his mind when, discovering she was pregnant, he had felt obliged to marry her.

'Which is how you ended up with me.'

The look Pierce turned on her made her heart jerk uncomfortably.

'I would have married you without any of my father's lectures. I don't need any instruction in my duties where my child is concerned.'

Duty, responsibility, concern for his child—she had always known that those were the reasons he had married her, but knowing didn't mean accepting, the bitter acknowledgement of the truth aggravating the sense of loss that was always with her. But at least he had married her, not left her to cope on her own as her unknown father had done to her mother.

'I'm grateful...'

The rest of her words died in her throat as Pierce rounded on her, blue eyes blazing.

'I don't want your *gratitude*, damn you!'

'Then what *do* you want from me?'

'I want—a wife.' His change of tone was unnerving. 'And as such you can start with my mother and the Christmas celebrations.'

'Christmas?' Natalie enquired hollowly. The undue haste with which their wedding had been arranged had meant that her contact with Alice Donellan had been kept to a strict minimum. What few meetings they had had been conducted in a tone of immaculate, if distinctly cool, politeness, and her new mother-in-law had as yet kept her opinion of her son's choice of bride very much to herself. 'She's coming here?'

'Of course she is.' Pierce frowned his displeasure at her shaken expression. 'The Manor is still her home, Nat. She's gone out of her way to consider us by moving out for the first couple of weeks so that we could have some time on our own together.'

Natalie couldn't suppress an involuntary wince as his intonation drove home how pointless an exercise he thought that had been. The relaxed ease of moments before had vanished, and they were back to the cold awkwardness that had prevailed ever since their wedding day.

'But now, of course, she wants to come back for the holidays. She'll be arriving on Tuesday—in good time for the carol service. And she'll be able to help you with all the arrangements for the party.'

'The party?' Forcing her mind to focus, Natalie remembered the party for the village children that the Manor laid on every year. It was always followed by a celebratory supper for the workers on the Manor estate.

Suddenly precisely what Pierce had said came home to her.

'To help me? Oh, but Pierce, I can't! Surely your mother—?'

'My mother organised the party for years. She'll be glad to hand it over to you. Besides, the whole village will be expecting to see you. For some of them, it will be their first glimpse of the new Lady of the Manor.'

But that wasn't her—that was the role Phillippa should have played. How could she stand at Pierce's side and accept everyone's congratulations, knowing he was only there out of *duty*?

'I can't—'

'You can and you will. You are my wife—'

'In name only!'

'You are my wife,' Pierce repeated, more emphatically this time, an ominous thread of danger lurking underneath the simple words like jagged rocks lying at the bottom of a deceptively still, calm sea. 'And you will act as such whenever the occasion demands. Above all else, you will never, ever give anyone reason to believe that our marriage is anything other than the whirlwind romance they believe it to be.'

'But—'

'But nothing, Natalie,' Pierce returned implacably. 'Everyone knows that my engagement to Phillippa was a mistake. I'll not have them thinking the same about my marriage.'

And there, of course, was the answer to the question that had plagued her earlier. Being rejected by Phillippa had been a dreadful blow to Pierce's masculine pride, particularly when it had been such a talking point in the village. To compensate for that, he had created the fiction that *their* marriage was a love match, the whirlwind romance he had called it. And that explained why he had not yet told his mother about the baby, and the carefully posed scene in front of the housekeeper just now. He had used her coldly and calculatedly in order to present the picture of his marriage that he wanted everyone to believe in.

'Is that clear?'

'Perfectly,' Natalie snapped. 'But how long will this farce last? After all—' for a brief moment her hand rested on her abdomen '—we can't pretend that my pregnancy doesn't exist for much longer. After New Year it will start to show...'

Pierce's blue eyes had followed her movement and as his gaze lingered where her hand touched Natalie had the strangest feeling that until that point he had actually forgotten about the baby. A second later she had rejected the idea as the foolishness it was. Of course he hadn't forgotten—it was the only reason he had married her in the first place!

'I don't intend to hide it from anyone,' Pierce said stiffly. 'It's just that I prefer to choose the right moment to tell everyone about it.'

'Of course you do!' The pain of knowing how coldly she was being manipulated made Natalie's voice bitter. 'It wouldn't fit in well with your careful fiction if people knew it was a shotgun wedding.'

'It was *not* a shotgun wedding!' For the first time, Pierce's dangerous calm broke, the cold fury in his eyes terrifying.

'It felt that way to me!' Natalie retorted with brittle flippancy. 'But however you describe it people are still going to think that you were forced—'

'Not if you play your part properly—which reminds me...'

Natalie knew what was coming, tensing in anticipation of the expected command.

'You'd better move your stuff into my room before my mother gets here. It won't look right if we're sleeping in separate beds.'

How she wished she dared refuse, but with Pierce in this mood she knew she didn't have the courage to defy him.

'Won't Mrs Newton say something?'

'Mrs Newton will keep her mouth shut if she knows what's wise,' Pierce declared harshly. 'And you can stop looking so horrified at the thought of sharing my bed; you've done it before, and if nothing else this move will give me a chance to put your mind at ease—on one score, at least.'

'And what's that?'

Every instinct Natalie possessed warned her that she wasn't going to like his answer, and the devilish grin he turned on her, a wicked gleam lighting his eyes, only aggravated the feeling.

'It will give me a chance to prove to you once and for all that, contrary to what you might think, I have no intention of letting you be a wife *in name only*. In fact, if Mrs Newton wasn't just about to announce that dinner is served I would prove it to you right here and now.'

'I—' Natalie swallowed hard, fighting the ambiguous feelings that warred inside her. 'You mean—'

'I mean that when I married you I fully intended it to be a proper marriage in every possible sense of the word—and that includes sharing my bed. I may have given you a few days to settle down, get used to your new home and all the other changes that have happened to you, but that was only a temporary concession—from tonight that privilege is withdrawn.'

'And will this be another temporary arrangement?'

'Oh, no.' Pierce shook his dark head decisively. 'On the contrary, this will be absolutely permanent. I want you in my bed tonight and every night for as long as this marriage lasts.'

And how long will that be? She couldn't ask the question out loud because she was afraid of the answer. Afraid he might say that once her baby was born and he was legally registered as the father he would have no further need of a marriage certificate, or indeed of his second-best wife. Deep down inside she knew that she had never expected this marriage to last, but she had no idea how she was going to cope when, as she felt was inevitable one day, Pierce finally told her it was all over.

CHAPTER EIGHT

'WELL, that went quite successfully.'

Alice Donellan sank down into a chair with a sigh of relief.

'More than *quite* successfully, Mother,' Pierce put in. 'I think you could say that the evening was a success all round, plain and simple— You did a brilliant job, Nat.'

Natalie basked in the warmth of his rare smile, letting it ease some of the tension that had gripped her all day. She had been a bag of nerves since the moment she had woken after a shallow and unsatisfactory night's sleep, terrified of the responsibility of the day ahead of her. The thought of acting as Lady of the Manor had been one that sent shivers down her spine simply to contemplate it, the problem aggravated by her mother-in-law's intimidating presence.

But in the end she had realised that she had been worrying unduly. From the moment she had set foot inside the village hall to see so many familiar faces, particularly the mothers and children from the school, it had been like coming home. She had been presented with a huge bouquet of flowers, a gesture that had brought tears to her eyes; everyone had been vociferous in their delight at her new status, and had made it plain how much it meant to them that 'one of their own' had made such a fairy-tale marriage.

'We knew that Phillippa wasn't the right type,' one woman had confided to her in a voice that couldn't help but carry across the room to where Pierce stood, slightly on the sidelines of the celebrations. 'Too full of herself by half.'

Natalie hadn't dared to look at Pierce, fearful of his reaction to that outspoken comment, and she had been frankly surprised when he had come to join her, staying by her side as she chatted casually to everyone who approached her.

'You're doing really well,' he'd murmured during a brief lull in the conversation. 'Handling this like a pro.'

His praise had had the effect of a rich wine on Natalie's spirits, making her eyes glow as she smiled up at him.

'It helps if you know everyone.'

'Are you tired, Nat?' Pierce asked her now, having obviously attributed her abstracted state to weariness. 'Don't let us keep you up.'

'Oh, no, I'm fine. I've coped with longer days at the school.'

If anything, he looked more tired than she felt, she thought, which brought back to her mind an idea that had crossed it earlier in the day, but which she had not paused to consider.

It had been early on, at the beginning of the afternoon, just after Pierce had come to her side, that she had taken a step back, allowing herself the luxury of simply watching him, letting her eyes rest on the lean, strong body, the gleaming dark hair, the forceful profile, that beautifully shaped mouth curving in a smile...

It had been that smile that had given him away. It had been the one she recognised as his social smile, the carefully polite one that hid his true feelings.

And so, looking at this strong, capable man who was her husband, Natalie had been forced to reflect on the comments Pierce had made about his father's insistence on the responsibilities that came with their position, his own comments about the village grapevine, and wonder if he still found being on show as much of a strain as he always had done.

As a result, when his hand had suddenly linked with hers, she'd had no idea just who was offering support to whom. But she hadn't questioned it, content simply to let her fingers lie in his as they worked the room as a couple, a team. For the first time she'd actually felt like that mythical person, Mrs Pierce Donellan, and for the brief space of one day had allowed herself to live the fantasy that their relationship was a real, solid-based thing.

So now, remembering, she managed a warm smile for this man who called himself her husband, letting her eyes linger hungrily on the tall, strong body in the black cord trousers and soft cotton shirt, its rich blue colour picking up and highlighting the sapphire lights of his eyes.

'It did go well, didn't it? Everyone seemed to enjoy themselves.'

'It seemed that way—and you looked spectacularly lovely all day.'

Natalie coloured sharply, fixing her eyes on the cup of tea Pierce had handed her—he was always scrupulous in remembering how badly coffee still affected her. She didn't know how to take the deep-voiced compliment.

Oh, she knew that the deep green velvet dress she wore, with its high neckline and softly flaring skirt, suited her dark colouring, its soft lines concealing the way that her figure was already beginning to change. But she had no idea whether Pierce's comment was genuinely meant or whether it was yet another ploy in his policy of convincing everyone—even his mother—that their marriage was a genuine love match.

'Well, you have very good taste,' she murmured, painfully aware of the fact that the dress and the jewellery she wore with it—a gold necklet and matching earrings—were all part of Pierce's Christmas present to her.

He had been almost obscenely generous to her, the pile of parcels under the huge tree in the hall taking her almost all of Christmas morning to open, and as well as the carefully chosen and brightly wrapped gifts he had provided her with a credit card in her married name, adding that it might be an idea if she used it to acquire a whole new wardrobe for the months to come.

At first, Natalie had been tempted to dig her heels in, declare that the clothes she had were perfectly adequate, but the realisation that everything was beginning to get just that little bit tight had combined with a very feminine need to look her best when she had to appear at Pierce's side to send her rushing out to the shops.

'And aren't you glad I persuaded you out of that stiff suit and into something more casual?'

Pierce nodded in agreement, his answering smile seeming to Natalie to have some echo of the unspoken closeness they had shared in the village hall.

'You were right about trying a new approach,' he said quietly. 'A bit more informality certainly lightened the atmosphere tonight. I don't think I've enjoyed one of those parties so much in a long time.'

Natalie's heart lifted at his words, a sense of joy singing through her.

'We'll have you acting as Father Christmas at the next one.' She laughed, but her attempt at a touch of humour fell spectacularly flat, Pierce's eyes suddenly darkening and a frown drawing his brows together in a worrying reminder that there was no guarantee that she would even be here for the next party.

By next December their child would be almost five months old. She would have served her purpose as provider of the needed heir, so would Pierce still want her around? Or would his determination to prove their relationship to be a whirlwind romance mean that before long it would behave just like that whirlwind and finally blow itself out?

'So, Natalie, when will you be leaving your position at the school?' Alice had clearly hunted for some topic of conversation, but the subject she had lighted upon was one guaranteed to set Natalie's teeth on edge, her eyes going to Pierce in sharp reproach.

'Mother overheard me telling your headmaster that you would be giving up your job,' he said, his bland response to her glare showing how unmoved he was by her anger at the way he had taken the decision out of her hands.

'Did you ask me if I wanted to become a kept woman?'

'Being a kept woman has nothing to do with anything.' Pierce's shrug dismissed her fury as unimportant. 'You'd have been leaving soon anyway.'

Natalie's teeth clenched tight against some violent retort. Obviously, as her pregnancy progressed, at some point she would have had to consider stopping teaching, or perhaps taking maternity leave, but in her own mind nothing had been finalised. Now Pierce had acted in this high-handed manner, taking things completely out of her hands, the arrogant way he had taken control of her life acting on her as a red rag did on a bull.

'And did you tell your mother *why* I'd be leaving?' she demanded.

Because, of course, that was what was behind it. The world could not be allowed to believe that the new Donellan bride could not be kept in the manner to which she'd soon grow accustomed, but even more important than that, in Pierce's mind at least, was the fact that nothing must jeopardise the health and safety of the baby she carried and her own feelings on the matter were of no concern to him.

'Not yet,' Pierce put in quietly, a note of warning shading the words.

'Well, isn't now as good a time as any?'

'*Nat!*' The warning was stronger now, but, driven by anger at the way her needs were being disregarded, she ignored it as she turned to Alice.

'I'll be handing in my notice just as soon as I go back after the Christmas holidays, and I'll be leaving before the end of the summer term.'

She wasn't going to be pushed into leaving any earlier, no matter what Pierce thought.

'You see, I decided not to take maternity leave any earlier, even though I'm entitled—'

Pierce's breath hissed in through his teeth as his mother's face changed revealingly. Natalie could almost read Alice's thoughts, hear her counting back dates, adding up figures, and, driven by a terrible imp of mischief, she resolved to leave her with no possible room for doubt.

'Because, after my baby's born in July, I plan to be a full-time mother.'

'Natalie, that's enough!' Pierce sounded coldly furious, but the hot blood that pounded through Natalie's veins obliterated reasonable thought, pushing her even further.

'And now I suppose you're even more convinced than ever that I'm the daughter-in-law from hell, the last person you would want to marry your precious son! I mean, the oh, so perfect Phillippa would never have been stupid or irresponsible enough to let herself get pregnant as the result of a hurried little one-night stand—'

'*Natalie*—I said that was enough!'

Pierce's roar, and his furious use of her full name, stopped her dead, the red haze evaporating swiftly from her mind, clearing her blurred vision and leaving it perfectly, painfully sharp. She saw the way the colour had left Alice's cheeks, and realised just what she had done. She didn't dare risk a look at Pierce; the reflection of his mood that showed on his mother's face was enough to have her swallowing hard.

'Yes, I suppose it is.' But, try as she might, she couldn't stop herself from adding, 'But isn't it much better to have it all out in the open? I hate living a lie.'

Out of the corner of her eye she saw the way that Pierce's hand clenched around his coffee-cup, warning her that what little remained of his patience was wearing very thin indeed. And now that her anger had ebbed so had her courage, and she knew she couldn't stay in the room a moment longer.

'I'll leave you to think about it!' she said unevenly, getting to her feet in an ungainly rush.

It was an effort to keep her head high, her back defiantly straight as she made her way to the door, painfully conscious of the two pairs of blue eyes, so very much alike, boring into her so that she fancied she could actually feel them scorching her skin. She had fully intended to leave it at that, and simply walk out without another word, but a sudden thought made her pause then swing round in the doorway.

'But just in case you're wondering if this baby really is Pierce's, or if, to add to all my other shortcomings, I'm guilty of trying to foist a cuckoo onto your precious family, then let me assure you that there's no room for doubt on that score. You see, unlike my mother—' better get that in before anyone else did '—or your son for that matter—I have only ever slept with one person. So, no matter how much you might wish it to be otherwise, my baby will most definitely be a Donellan through and through—your grandchild—as any blood tests you might demand would prove one hundred per cent!'

And that, she thought with something close to hysteria, was very possibly the best exit line she was going to get, and besides, she didn't think what was left of her composure would hold out any longer. And so she turned on her heel swiftly and almost ran from the room, taking the stairs two at a time in her haste to get away.

Pierce wasn't far behind her. She had barely had time to recover her breath, let alone her composure, before he was in the room with her, blue eyes blazing and the muscles around his mouth drawn tight in a way that made her heart sink.

'What the hell was all that about?' he demanded, leaning back against the closed door so that there was no way she could escape if she was foolish enough to try.

'I don't know why you're making a fuss!' Natalie tried to brazen it out. 'I only told the truth and it's time that your mother knew it. I can't be any more of a disappointment to her than I already am to you.'

'Disappointment is not the word!' Pierce flung at her through clenched teeth.

'Well, too bad—it's me you married and I'm not Phillippa!'

'Do you think I don't know that?' Pierce raked both hands through the black silk of his hair and drew in a deep, uneven breath. 'You're definitely not Phillippa, but you are my wife and the mother of my child—no matter how that came about—and when Ma's calmed down she'll accept you as such.'

'Is she very angry?' Natalie's own temper had ebbed away, leaving her feeling rather shaken, as she often did after one of her outbursts.

'Do you really want me to answer that?'

'Oh, dear.' Sliding to the edge of the bed, she felt for her shoes with her feet. 'Perhaps I'd better go and—'

'Don't do anything more! My reputation is already in ruins.'

That brought her up short. '*Your* reputation?'

Pierce nodded, a wry twist to his lips.

'Believe me, my mother is none too pleased at the thought of her only son being cast in the role of seducer of young virgins.'

'Seducer—but you didn't!'

'Didn't I? I am nine years older than you, after all— more than that in experience, as you made only too plain just now. I should have been more careful—acted more responsibly. So in my mother's eyes I'm well and truly cast as the villain in all this.'

'But that's not what I meant to happen!'

'Isn't it?' His sudden cynicism was dark and disturbing. 'Isn't that how you and your mother saw it all along—that no good could come from any association between you and—?'

'No—you were the one who didn't want to mess around with—with the likes of me.' Bitterness rang in her voice as she threw his own words back at him.

'And who would have—then?' Pierce threw back at her, making her frown in confusion.

'I don't understand.'

'Think about it, Nat—on the one hand I had my parents drumming into me the responsibilities of my position, and on the other there was your mother breathing fire and brimstone and threatening everlasting torment if I so much as laid a finger on you.'

'I never knew she said anything to you—only—'

'That she made her fears plain where you were concerned. Of course she did; she didn't want you to endure the sort of life she'd led—and back then you certainly were a complication I could well do without.'

'Thanks for the compliment!'

'Do you want me to lie? Goddammit, Nat! I was barely twenty-eight myself. The company was just taking off. I had money, my freedom—I didn't want to tie myself down in any way. All right—I'll admit I was tempted. You were ever so slightly tipsy and gorgeous as hell.'

He moved from the door and sat down on the bed beside her. The sudden sidelong glance from those blue eyes was filled with wry humour, matching the smile that curled the corners of his mouth.

'You didn't think I'd noticed you'd grown up? I'll be honest—I hadn't, until then. But that night you were dressed up, made up—grown up—and I was tempted.'

Once more the long fingers raked through the thick darkness of his hair.

'God, I was tempted! But I could never have lived with myself if I'd done anything about it. For one thing, I'd have proved all your mother's dire predictions justified.'

'And now?'

Natalie didn't know whether she was relieved or desolated that he had omitted a vital element in his recollection of the events of her eighteenth birthday. He had never once mentioned her declaration of love. Obviously, he had taken her at her word when she had claimed it was just the result of a foolish teenage crush and had forgotten it. Either that or the thought of it and the possibility that there might be some residue of the feeling lingering deep in her mind was such an embarrassment to him that he was deliberately avoiding bringing up the subject again.

'Now?' Pierce looked deep into her eyes. 'Now I have proved your mother right—but at least I'm doing something about it.'

'All right, you don't have to hit me over the head with it,' Natalie muttered ungraciously, those four words 'I had my freedom' echoing inside her head, forcing her to face just what he had lost because of her. A forced marriage had been what he had most feared, and that was just what she'd pushed him into. 'I didn't want this to happen any more than you did.'

'But now that it has happened, surely we can both be adult enough to make the best of it? One thing I'll promise you, Nat. I'll never abandon you as your father left your mother. This baby will always know who its father is, and you'll never want for anything.'

Except for love, a lonely little voice murmured inside Natalie's head. They were back once again to duty and responsibility—but at least it was mixed with something else—the desire he had admitted to both now and in the past.

'As you said yourself, it took two to make this baby, Pierce,' she said gruffly, her voice sounding as if it came from a raw and painful throat. 'Your mother should know that. In fact—'

Pushing her feet into her shoes, she got up from the bed in a rush.

'I'll go down and tell her so.'

'Oh, no, you won't!'

Pierce launched himself across the room after her, strong hands closing over her shoulders, pulling her unceremoniously back onto the bed.

'I think you've done enough damage for one night. You leave my mother to me. In fact, it's more than time you were in bed and resting. Remember that baby you're carrying—and after this evening you're going to need all your energy—'

'To work out my notice?'

'If you must. I was thinking more on the lines of coping with my mother in the role of doting grandmother— You needn't look so sceptical!' he added, with an unexpected and devastating grin. 'My mother has dreamed of having grandchildren for a long time. It was always a terrible disappointment to her that she didn't have more family of her own. I told you about my brother who died—he wasn't the only baby she lost. She also had two miscarriages before that, and a stillborn daughter after me.'

Which went a long way towards explaining Alice Donellan—and her son, Natalie reflected. Naturally, after such tragedies, Pierce's mother would want nothing but the best for her only child. And Pierce, as the only living offspring, would feel the burden of duty that his parents had insisted on all the more because he was the only one to shoulder it.

'And since my father died she's fixed on the idea of my children giving new meaning to her life.'

Suddenly Pierce moved closer beside her on the bed, one of the hands that held her prisoner sliding down from her shoulder to rest very lightly on the soft swell of her stomach.

'So, you see, this baby will be very precious to her— almost as much as it will be to me.'

Looking at his downbent head, seeing the way his features had softened, his gaze fixed on the long, powerful fingers splayed out on the green velvet of her dress, Natalie felt her heart turn over in love and longing. At least she could give him the child he so wanted. In this one way, her marriage was not the second best it was in every other aspect.

'Pierce—'

She wanted desperately to tell him how she felt but her courage failed her when Pierce's mood changed with jarring abruptness, the smile he turned on her distant and impersonal as he got swiftly to his feet.

'Right.'

His voice matched his demeanour—crisp and unemotional; business as usual. She was the source of his major investment in the future, and, like any shrewd financier, he wanted to safeguard his assets.

'Time you were in bed and asleep.'

The kiss he dropped onto her forehead was as brusque and meaningless as the smile, making her heart clench on a spasm of pain.

'I'd better get downstairs and face the music.'

Left alone, Natalie went through the motions of getting undressed and into bed with the lifelessness of an automaton, all her energy seeming to have drained away in the moment that Pierce had kissed her. That kiss had meant nothing. It hadn't even been the sort of affectionate peck on the cheek he might have given her if they had simply been platonic friends. Even though she had his ring on her finger, to Pierce she was still nothing more than the woman who carried his child.

His child—the baby was all that Pierce cared about. He was kind and considerate towards her, made sure she had everything she needed, at least as far as her material needs were concerned, but that was all. As a result she felt more and more like some valuable thoroughbred mare that had to be cosseted and cared for because of the precious life she carried within her.

She was even fooling herself with thoughts of the desire he had felt for her—*had* seeming to be the operative word. Even Pierce's decree that she move into his room had been just part of the pretence he was prepared to go through in order to convince people that their marriage was a real one; it was as much of a sham as everything else. They might sleep together, but that was all. Since she had moved into his bed, Pierce had never touched her, more often than not making some excuse to stay downstairs working until she was asleep.

But that at least was something she could change, couldn't she? Pierce might not love her, but if she could revive the passion that had flared between them it would give her another advantage, something to build on, and then when she had had the baby...

Such thoughts kept her from sleep, and when Pierce finally came up to bed much later she waited until he had undressed and was lying beside her before she turned towards him.

'Pierce...'

'Still awake?' He sounded surprised and, worryingly, rather tense.

'I couldn't sleep. How's your mother?'

'Probably dreaming of baby clothes and prams. She went to bed half an hour ago.'

But he had delayed, staying downstairs—until he hoped she was asleep? The stab of pain that thought brought firmed her resolve.

'You know, in all this talk of responsibility, there's one you've forgotten.'

Wriggling closer, Natalie let her head rest on the hard strength of his shoulder, running her fingers down the strong lines of his chest.

'One duty you've definitely been neglecting,' she murmured in mock petulance.

The long body beside her stiffened, his swiftly indrawn breath telling her that he was far from indifferent to the touch of her wandering fingers.

'Nat...'

She forced herself to ignore the husky warning note in his voice, letting her hand trace tiny, erotic circles in the dark hair her fingers encountered before moving downwards again, drawing an invisible line around his narrow waist.

'Nat...' His voice was less confident now, and there was a definite shake on her name, one that made her smile secretly as she pressed her lips to the warm satin of his skin.

'I'm sure your mother would not be at all pleased if she knew how neglected I'd been feeling.'

'But I— What about the baby? I wouldn't want to harm—'

'You won't.'

For a second Natalie had to grit her teeth against an angry retort. The baby—always the baby! But even as the bitter thought sparked in her mind she sensed the change in Pierce, a very different sort of tension now in the hard length that pressed so close against her, and she felt her own hunger grow in response.

'I'm not your mother, Pierce,' she assured him softly. 'And nothing is going to harm our baby—at least nothing you can do. But they do say that even in the womb a child knows if its mother is feeling unhappy or upset, and just lately I've been feeling very lonely and neglected.'

That had him turning to her in concern.

'Nat! I never meant—I didn't want to force myself—'

'Oh, Pierce,' she broke in sharply. 'Don't you know that force doesn't come into it?'

With a rough sound in his throat, he reached for her, crushing her close, and as his mouth came down hard on hers her heart soared, because she knew that, for now at least, she was central to his world, all-important in one way if nothing else.

For the very first time she found she could respond to Pierce in the fullest way, neither frightened by her own need nor disturbed by it in any way, and as his hands closed over her swollen breasts she pressed every inch of her body against the hard, lean length of his, making him groan urgently.

'Nat—we should take this slowly—carefully...'

'There's no need to be careful,' she whispered huskily, her breath feathering against his ear. 'And besides, I don't want that.'

The shudder that was his response to her soft words made her smile in the darkness, feeling the hunger in his hands, the need that communicated itself through his fingertips, the heat of his mouth.

'You don't?'

'No way.'

'Then show me, Nat—show me what you do want.'

Hearing the thickness of passion that filled his words, she laughed softly and drew his hands to her, empowered by a dizzying awareness of her own sensuality, of the answering desire she could awaken in him. It gave her the most devastating sense of liberty, of freedom to touch him where and how she pleased, and she took full advantage of it, letting her exploring hands wander over every inch of his heated body, feeling the satin warmth of his flesh quiver beneath her touch, his breathing quickening, becoming ragged and uneven.

'Nat—' Her name was a raw sound in his throat, more revealing than any declaration of feeling, an admission of the true power of her femininity. 'Nat, I can't—'

'You don't have to,' she told him, her hips lifting towards him, inviting the union they both craved, her own thoughts spinning out of control as his strong fingers caressed the most intimate part of her body until she writhed against him in mute demand.

Time no longer existed; the world seemed to fade into a burning haze. The only reality was here, in this bed, with this man whose body was one with hers, whose breathing matched her every gasp, his voice her every cry. It was the most perfect completeness, the sensation of total unity so sharp it was an agony of delight as well as an ecstasy of feeling, and each movement, each kiss, each caress added to that sense, building into a mind-shattering explosion of pure joy that made her sob his name out loud, hearing her own on his lips at almost the same second.

It was a long time before she was capable of anything beyond feeling, before the shivers of passion subsided and her sated body could finally lie still in the heavy aftermath of pleasure. But when her mind would finally function again she knew that Pierce lay beside her, his long body so indolent with satisfaction that he reminded her of a cat stretched blissfully before a fire, too completely content even to purr.

'Like I said,' he murmured, his voice rich with darkly sensual satisfaction, 'never, ever a wife in name only.'

And Natalie was grateful for the way that the darkness hid her face, not knowing which was uppermost in her mind—the deep, primitive satisfaction that came from knowing that she could ignite such a blazing passion in him, or the sharper, more uncomfortable sense of loss at the thought that that was *all* he felt.

Still, at least they had this, she told herself. At least this was something she could give him, something that brought them together, forged links of passion between them. She didn't know if it would be enough to create a future from, but at least it was a start, a foundation, and perhaps one day something more could grow from it.

CHAPTER NINE

'MRS DONELLAN...' The housekeeper's tone was strangely hesitant. 'There's—someone to see you. I told him you were resting but he was most insistent. He said it was very important.'

'I'm not expecting anyone.' Natalie frowned her confusion. 'What's he like, May?'

Mrs Newton's face said it all. 'He's not from the village,' she replied carefully. 'And he said you hadn't seen him for a long time.'

'Really?'

Now she was intrigued. She was also bored out of her head, as she had been for weeks now, it seemed, and the thought of some distraction was welcome.

'I suppose I'd better see him—what name did he give?'

'Wilton—David Wilton. Should I tell Mr Pierce too?'

'Did he ask for my husband? No? Then I don't think there's any point in disturbing him.' Natalie smoothed the blue flowered cotton of her dress over the swell of her stomach, much more prominent now after eight months. 'After all, we both know what he's like when he's interrupted, don't we?'

She knew she was on safe ground there. Ever since Pierce had abandoned his trips to London, opting instead for working from home in order to be close at hand as her pregnancy advanced, both Natalie and the housekeeper had entered into a conspiracy of amused tolerance of the way he reacted if anyone ventured into his study during working hours. He was like a bear that someone had prodded with a red-hot poker on such occasions, and the two women had found it simpler to make sure that the minor problems of domestic life were dealt with without involving him.

Unless, of course, the problem was something to do with the baby, Natalie added wryly to herself as Mrs Newton disappeared to fetch the visitor. Then he seemed to have a powerful sixth sense, an intuitive awareness of everything that was happening, even if it was well away from him, behind closed doors. He had the knack of appearing out of the blue, without being called, just when he was needed.

And he had been needed once or twice, she recalled, getting out of her chair and stretching to ease the ache in her back that had plagued her day and night in the past weeks. There had been the time in early February when she had endured a wretched couple of weeks with a nasty dose of flu, and only last month, as a result of no longer being able to see her feet now that the bump of her pregnancy was so big, she had missed her footing on the stairs and fallen awkwardly.

She had only been five steps from the bottom, and hadn't really hurt herself, but it had been as if her movements were being tracked on some inner radar screen of Pierce's mind, and his study door had been flung open before she had even hit the ground. Seconds later, she had been gathered up into strong, protective arms, Pierce's face white with shocked concern.

And then there was the change in her blood pressure. 'Nothing to panic about,' the doctor had assured her. 'But all the same you'd do better to be careful. I want you to take things very easy.'

And that, of course, Pierce had translated as doing absolutely nothing. Which was all very well for him, but with the bright sunshine of a late June day outside, and the prospect of another four weeks or so confined to her bed or an armchair, it was driving Natalie up the wall. So now, when the door opened again, she turned swiftly in response, grateful for any diversion.

'Mr Wilton—do come in.'

She realised now just why Mrs Newton had seemed so concerned. This David Wilton was not the sort of caller that might have been expected at the Manor. His clothes were well worn and shabby, his shoes cracked and down at heel. He was perhaps four or five inches taller than Natalie herself and excess weight had blurred the outlines of his body, and he had lank dark hair that was thinning rapidly. All in all, his appearance was that of someone who was definitely down on his luck, something about the look in his eyes making her wonder if she would have been wiser to let Mrs Newton tell Pierce after all.

'What can I do for you?'

'Well, perhaps it's more what I can do for you. You don't know me, do you? No—well...' He sighed deeply running one hand over the shiny skin of his bald patch 'Why should you? I haven't been in your life for years. But I'd know you anywhere—those eyes—that hair You're the image of your mother. You're definitely my Natty Dread.'

'Natty Dread? That's a song, isn't it? Reggae?'

He nodded without speaking, but with a strange smil lifting the corners of his mouth as he seemed to wait fo her to go on, add something to her remark. And, sur prisingly, there *were* other echoes in her mind, a sort o swirling sense of unease, as if someone had suddenl stirred up the silt lying at the bottom of a pond, cloudin the water.

'Natty...' As she spoke the name again, it seemed as if the muddied water cleared slightly so that she glimpsed something vaguely, blurrily. 'It's a nickname.' The man before her was nodding in agreement. '*My* nickname! Someone used to call me that.'

'That's right. Look, perhaps it will help if I tell you that I came back to Ellerby looking for Nora.' His expression became sombre and he touched the back of one hand to his eye. 'Of course I wasn't to know she'd passed away. At first I went to where we used to live in Mill Street, and they told me to try Holme Road. The neighbours there—'

But Natalie wasn't really listening. 'Where *we* lived— Mill Street—you said where *we* lived!'

'That's right. Oh, Natty, don't you know who I am?'

Did he mean what she thought he did? *Could* he be? She had thought that her mother had said Hilton, but Nora had been in a haze of delirium, very weak, her words muttered, so that it was impossible to be sure that she hadn't said *Wilton*.

'But why should you recognise me—or even want to see me? I admit that I wasn't a very good parent to you, or partner to Nora. But I want to make that up to you. And now—especially now.'

Natalie clutched at a nearby table for support, her head whirling frantically.

'Who—are you?'

'Oh, Natty, darling, you must know! You don't need to ask—'

'But *you* do need to answer her,' broke in a crisp, cool voice, bringing David Wilton whirling round to where Pierce, coolly elegant in a soft white short-sleeved shirt and pale grey trousers, lounged in the doorway. Mrs

Newton must have acted on her feelings after all, and told him of the visitor.

'Pierce—' She couldn't gather her thoughts to do more than speak his name as a sharply assessing sapphire-blue gaze swept over her, taking in her flushed cheeks and over-bright eyes, a dark frown crossing his face.

'Sit down before you fall down, Nat!' he barked, only slightly softening the imperiousness of the command by the way he moved across the room to take her arms and guide her into a chair.

Shock and confusion made her respond to his command with the mindless compliance of a string puppet, and as she sank into the soft cushions Pierce positioned himself beside her, on the chair-arm, facing David Wilton across the room.

'You must be Pierce—Natty's husband. I'm delighted to meet you.'

Wilton moved forward exuberantly, his hand held out in greeting, only to be frozen into stillness by the icy glare from those cold blue eyes.

'And who might you be?' Each word was formed with a disdainful precision.

'Dave Wilton at your service.' It had taken him only seconds to recover from Pierce's obvious hostility, but a watchful gleam in his eyes showed that he was very definitely sizing up the opposition.

'And what can we do for you, Mr Wilton?' That 'we' was very subtly emphasised.

'Well—I take it you are the Pierce Donellan my Natty married?'

'*Your* Natty?' Pierce echoed with cool contempt, the Lord of the Manor at his most arrogant.

'That's right.' Wilton was nodding enthusiastically, apparently oblivious to the bite of acid in the other man's tone. 'My little girl.'

'Are you claiming to be Natalie's father?'

He didn't believe a word of it, his tone said only too plainly, making Natalie wince inside. She had never seen Pierce like this before. This must be what he was like in the business world. This sort of hardness had won him his reputation for being totally ruthless.

'I'm not claiming! I *am*—'

'And, of course, you'd be able to prove that?'

'Well, look at me—and at her: brown eyes, dark hair— well, what's left of it—'

'But do you have any *proof*?' Pierce persisted mercilessly.

'No documents, if that's what you mean. Nora and I never made things official.' A confiding note slid into his voice. 'I'll be honest with you, mate, I wasn't the best of bets for any woman in those days, not the sort to settle down. But for Nora I tried. I managed nearly three years, but in the end the wanderlust got the better of me. I always meant to come back—never forgot Nora—but somehow the years just slipped away. You can imagine what a dreadful shock it was for me to find she'd died.'

For a couple of seconds, nicotine-stained fingers covered the brown eyes and David Wilton shook his head sorrowfully. In her chair, Natalie made an instinctive movement. If this *was* her father—

But Pierce's hand tightened bruisingly on her shoulder, holding her still when she would have got to her feet to offer comfort. After a moment's silence, Wilton cleared his throat noisily.

'Well, it's too late now for Nora, but not for my Natty—and of course she needs me more than ever now.'

'And why is that?'

Natalie would have sworn that it was impossible for Pierce's tone to become any more coldly hostile, but somehow he managed it, the ominous note in his voice making her shift uneasily in her seat.

'Well, with a kiddy of her own on the way—every girl needs her family around at such a time.'

'If you are family.'

'Of course I am. Natty, tell him—you must know!'

'Do you, Nat?'

'I—'

Natalie felt as if she was caught in the middle of some appalling nightmare, except that she wasn't asleep and so there was no hope of ever waking up and breaking free from it. Her wide brown eyes went from one man to the other, from Pierce's hard, set face to the more expressive features of the older man, whose dark eyes, so like her own, seemed to plead with her to believe him.

Was he her father? Could he be the man she had so longed to know, the part of her life that had been missing for so many years? He certainly wasn't the fantasy figure that had filled her imagination, but those images had been just dreams.

'I remember being called Natty Dread . . .'

But shouldn't she feel something? If his blood flowed in her veins . . .

'I don't know!' It was a cry of distress, sharpened by a twist of discomfort as her baby kicked as if in response.

'Nat—it's all right—'

But Pierce's soothing words were overlaid by Wilton's blustering reproach.

'But Natty, darling, you must know—you must remember! Look, your birthday is September the ninth, and for a present I bought you your first puppy—Mr Punch—a Jack Russell.'

He had her attention now—and Pierce's—his eyes fixed so intently on the older man's face that Natalie almost expected to see his skin scorch under the powerful scrutiny.

'Of course, after Punch there was Toby—'

Natalie's mind reeled. Mr Punch—Toby—he knew so much...

'Toby?' It was Pierce who spoke, his voice sharp as a blade.

'Oh, yes, he was to replace poor Mr Punch when he was run over.' The dark eyes were turned on Natalie again. 'You were brokenhearted.'

She could only nod silently, tears streaming down her cheeks. Her father... She would have got up then and gone to him, but Pierce still held her in a fierce grip, his fingers digging into her shoulders.

'Mr Wilton.' He was imposing a ruthless control on himself and his voice, Natalie realised with a sense of shock, holding himself back every bit as forcefully as he was restraining her. 'Just how did you find out about Natalie? How did you know where to come looking for her?'

'Oh, well, that was the most amazing stroke of luck. Would you believe it was in a newspaper? My second night here, after I'd learned poor Nora was dead, I bought myself some fish and chips, and there, in the paper they were wrapped in, was a report of the wedding. Can you credit it—?'

'No.' The single syllable was flat and inimical. 'No, I wouldn't credit it. Oh, I believe you read the report in

the paper, and I believe you once lived in Mill Street—
but you're not Natalie's father and I want you out of
here now!'

'Pierce—no!' Natalie turned to him in shocked
distress.

'Natalie, you're not thinking straight. Believe me...'

Bright and clear, those blue eyes burned into her dazed
brown ones as if willing her to see what he did. When
he looked at her like that, she would believe anything,
but for this she needed more than blind trust.

'The newspaper—and you told me yourself about Mr
Punch. Think...'

Think. Reaching back into her memories, she recalled
the day she had met Pierce out walking the family's dog,
and telling him that she had once had her own pet—
heard her own voice saying, 'Mr Punch was killed by a
car when I was four.'

'Mr Wilton.' It took an effort to make the words
audible. 'Exactly when was I born?'

'I told you...' There was more than a touch of bravado
in his response. 'September.'

'No, the *year*.' Pierce's nod of satisfaction told her
she was on the right track.

'Let me see—you're twenty-two, so—'

'Pierce, make him go.' Natalie's voice was dull and
low. 'He's not my father.'

'Eh? Now look—just because I don't recall—'

'You don't recall anything.' Pierce's words slashed
through the blustering protest. 'Because you're not who
you say you are. A real father would never forget the
year his daughter was born. You see, the newspaper
report you read got it wrong. They printed my wife's
age as twenty-two when in fact she's two years older—
and if you were around when Mr Punch died, and by

your own admission you were only with Nora for three years—'

'Oh, all right, damn you!' Wilton's face had changed so completely that Natalie barely recognised him as the hesitant, smiling man who had first come into the room. 'So I tried it on—who wouldn't? I mean, I knew that kid when she was nothing—had nothing—but now she's come up in the world. You're loaded, and—'

'And you thought you'd try and get your grubby hands on some of my money by claiming to be my father-in-law?' Pierce flung the words at him as if simply speaking them contaminated him.

'You can spare it.' The reply came sullenly.

'And what about the effect on Natalie? How do you think she'd feel, thinking that her father only wanted her because she was rich? Oh, get out of here!'

Eyes blazing, he strode to the door, flinging it open as he turned a look of total contempt on the older man.

'Get out before I throw you out! And if you're wise you'll get out of Ellerby too, because if I ever see you again I won't be responsible for my actions!'

Natalie barely saw David Wilton leave; the tears that had dried as she'd concentrated on the questions Pierce had asked and the replies he received now could not be held in check any longer, and she bent her head, burying her face in her hands. The aching emptiness of loss seemed so much worse because she had briefly come so close to filling it.

'Natalie! Oh, Nat, don't!'

Strong arms came round her, warm and protective, and she was gathered close against the comforting support of his chest, held tightly yet gently as the storm of emotion broke over her.

'Sweetheart, don't cry—you know I can't bear to see you in tears—I never could, right from the moment I saw you lying by the side of the road with mud all over your face, and your leg in such a mess. You were trying so hard to be brave, but one big tear had made a shiny trail through the dirt, and I just wanted to rescue you— wave a magic wand and put it all right.'

'Instead of which, despite your look of concern and gentle words, I remember you couldn't resist saying something on the lines of, "For God's sake, brat, what the hell sort of mess have you got yourself into now?"'

'Did I?' Pierce's tone was wry. 'I never was very good at expressing how I really felt.'

And just what did that mean? Natalie's breath seemed to catch in her throat, her thoughts suddenly diverted onto new and very different paths. Easing herself back in his arms, she didn't dare look into his face for fear she mightn't read there what she hoped to find, and instead she focused her blurred gaze on his chest and on the shirt that until a few moments ago had been immaculately clean.

'Oh, look what I've done!' Ineffectually she rubbed at the mascara smudges with her fingers. 'Pierce, I've ruined it!'

His careless shrug dismissed her concern.

'It'll wash; and if it doesn't, what's a shirt between friends?' His laughter was touched with something Natalie couldn't interpret. 'Isn't this the point where I'm supposed to pull a spotless white handkerchief from my pocket? If so, I'm afraid I'm a hopeless failure as a romantic hero because all I can offer are these.'

Reaching across to a box of tissues on a nearby table, he pulled out a handful, giving her a couple before using the rest to wipe her face with a gentleness that was as

magical as it was unexpected, warming her heart enough
to ease some of the aching emptiness.

'I must look such a mess.'

'Your cheeks are a little red, and those beautiful eyes
rather swollen, but that's all— He's not worth it, Nat!'
he added with sudden sharpness. 'He's nothing but a
cheap crook and a con man.'

'He could have been my father.'

'But he wasn't.'

His brusqueness hurt. He didn't understand, but how
could he? He had never lived with that gap in his life.

'Well, of course you were against him from the start,
just because he was obviously scruffy and down at heel.
I suppose he wasn't good enough for you—not the sort
of person you'd want as grandfather to your precious
child!'

'Not the sort I'd want as a father-in-law, certainly.'

'But what if he *had* been—?'

'Natalie, are you so desperate for a father—a family—
that you'll grab the first claimant that comes along, no
matter how dreadful they are?' When she couldn't
answer he added sombrely, 'Was that why you married
me?'

Not knowing exactly how the question was being
asked, Natalie chose the words to answer it with great
care.

'It had a good deal to do with it.'

'Well, thank you very much!'

'And just what are you so indignant about?' The un-
fairness of his anger piqued her into throwing the words
into his dark, set face. 'After all, wasn't that precisely
why *you* married *me*?'

Pierce's head went back as if he had been struck hard in the face and something she had never seen before flared in his eyes.

'Well—yes—I would have felt I had a duty to marry any woman who was pregnant with my child, so that did influence my decision.'

'I'll bet it did! You couldn't have your first choice, but you'd settle for a very second best if she brought you a baby as a job lot.'

'Oh, for God's sake, Natalie!' The force of Pierce's explosion shocked her. '*You* are my wife. It's working out quite well, isn't it? Even my mother is coming round to the idea.'

'Well, yes...'

Natalie had to acknowledge that, as the baby grew, so her relationship with Alice Donellan developed slowly too. Now that she understood more about the older woman's past, it was easier to understand her, and although they weren't yet anything like friends they could at least tolerate each other much more. And only the previous week Alice had surprised her by confiding in her.

'I have to admit that, at the beginning, I had my doubts about you and Pierce, but things are beginning to turn out better than I ever hoped. You see, I know my son, Natalie. I love him dearly, but, let's face it, his record with women hasn't been exactly exemplary. I'd be the first to admit that until now he hasn't shown the sort of commitment one would want in a marriage.'

Natalie had only been able to manage an inarticulate murmur in response, but Alice hadn't seemed to need her contribution.

'I used to think it was his reaction against my husband's insistence on him shouldering his duties—his love

life was one area in which he could be irresponsible—
but now I see that he just hadn't met the right woman.
You're the first he's ever stayed with for more than a
few months. For the first time in his life he's actually
settling down.'

'But your mother doesn't know that the baby is the
only reason why we married,' Natalie said now. Alice
didn't know that Pierce wasn't faithful to her through
choice, but because of the baby and Phillippa's rejection
of him.

'Natalie, have I ever given you cause to think I regret
marrying you?'

'No...' He'd been attentive, considerate, generous,
flatteringly passionate before she'd got too big, kindness
itself when she'd been unwell. But then, as he had just
admitted, he would have felt such a duty to any woman
he had got pregnant, and, being Pierce, he would have
settled himself to making the best of it. But we both
know why I'm here.'

'And that is?'

'You know! All I am to you is an incubator for your
baby.'

Her voice broke on the words. Saying them aloud like
this made it all seem so much worse, so that she no longer
knew if she could continue with this sham marriage or
not.

'You can't have a child without a woman to carry
it—'

'How dare you?' Once more she was shocked by the
dark fury in Pierce's face. 'How the bloody hell dare
you accuse me—?'

'No—how dare *you* marry me when—? Oh!'

She broke off in shock, her hands going to the swell
of her stomach.

'Nat!' Immediately, Pierce was all concern. 'What's wrong?'

'Nothing,' she managed shakily when she could speak. 'It's just the baby—it gave me an almighty kick. I've never felt anything like it. Oh! There it goes again!'

Impulsively she reached out to grab both of Pierce's hands, spreading them over the bulge under the fine blue cotton of her dress, needing to share the moment.

'Can you feel it?'

'No—I—Oh, God!'

A look of sheer delight crossed his face, wiping away all the anger of moments before.

'It's fantastic!'

Suddenly he turned to her, his hands coming up to cup her face, holding her very gently as he leaned forward to press a lingering kiss on her lips—a kiss that in spite of its slow intensity had nothing sexual in it. It couldn't even have been described as simply affectionate, but was somehow very different from any kiss he had ever given her before, touched with a special sort of feeling that made her head spin, set her blood singing in her veins.

'Thank you for this, Natalie,' he said simply.

And then she knew that her fears of earlier had been unfounded. She *could* continue with this marriage. She could endure anything if only once in a while he would look at her like that, kiss her as he had just done. If he did, she wouldn't ask for more.

'That's what friends are for.' She took refuge behind flippancy.

Pierce didn't like it; his dark frown told her that.

'You—referred to us as friends—just now. Surely we can be that?' she asked anxiously, struggling to ignore another uncomfortable twinge around her abdomen.

Disturbingly, Pierce hesitated, the frown deepening as he appeared to consider.

'To tell you the truth, Nat, I find it increasingly difficult to define just what we are to each other. I don't really think we can be *friends*.'

'No?' It was impossible to conceal her pain fully. 'But Pierce—'

Pierce shook his dark head in rejection of her protest.

'Nat, friends are supposed to be platonic—they aren't supposed to have the sort of feelings I have for you.'

'What sort of feelings?'

'You know—you don't need me to tell you. I've only got to look at you to want you. You're so beautiful—'

'Hardly!' Natalie interjected. 'That I don't believe.'

'Have you looked in the mirror lately?' Pierce demanded. 'Motherhood agrees with you—your hair shines, your skin glows—there's a wonderful serenity about you...'

Not right now there wasn't, Natalie thought privately. Her heart was beating nineteen to the dozen, flooding her face with colour, and the baby seemed determined to kick her black and blue.

'I'm not beautiful,' she managed. 'It's certainly not a word anyone has ever used to describe me. Homely perhaps, or nice—but not beautiful. Someone like Phillippa—'

Too late she saw her mistake and wished the inflammatory name back.

'Leave Phillippa out of this,' Pierce growled. 'She's nothing to do with us.'

If only she could believe that, how much easier life would be. But the other woman was always there, coming between them. She knew she was not Pierce's first choice—

But at that moment her thought processes shattered as she struggled with another spasm of pain, the dreadful realisation hitting home that this was not just the baby kicking, it was much more than that—

'Pierce!' It came out on a gasp of shock.

'What is it?' As before, he was alert at once, warm fingers lacing with hers.

'I think—the baby—'

'But you can't! The doctor said three weeks or more.'

'I—don't think your child is going to wait for the designated date!' Natalie managed through teeth clenched against another spasm of pain.

'But it's too early—or could the dates be wrong?'

'Pierce!'

She was driven to shaky laughter by the sight of this man who had always seemed so coolly capable, so totally in control, reduced to such a state of panic that he was being supremely illogical.

'If there's one thing we can be sure of it's the damn date on which this baby was conceived!'

They were the last words she managed. Within seconds, all possibility of coherent thought had fled from her mind, driven away by the waves of pain that picked her up and swept her away from the physical world into a haze of burning delirium through which she was only vaguely aware of Pierce yelling instructions at someone, of doors opening and the sound of running footsteps.

Then she was being lifted, carried, held so very gently and yet so securely that she knew a deep confidence, a certainty that she would be taken care of. She had a blurred impression of a blue sky and a brightly burning sun for a moment before she was placed carefully in the back of a car, Pierce sliding in beside her as the powerful engine began to roar.

'Hold on, sweetheart,' his voice, rough and husky, murmured reassuringly in her ear. 'Just a few minutes.'

She couldn't see, couldn't think, could barely even breathe properly, but through the pain and the distress one thing registered clearly. She was intensely aware of the strength of the warm arms that held her, their power communicating comfort, support and caring far more eloquently than any words could ever have done, and she clenched her hands around his, unaware of the way her nails were digging into his skin.

'Pierce,' she whispered through gasping, rawly indrawn breaths. 'Pierce—don't leave me—please—don't leave—'

'Never,' that deep, harsh voice assured her on a note of husky sincerity. 'Never in all my life...'

Hard fingers gripped hers, tightening in empathic response as another contraction ripped through her body, and with his words echoing over and over inside her head she clung onto the strength of his hands as if they were her only lifeline in a world that had suddenly gone terribly, agonisingly mad.

CHAPTER TEN

'MORE flowers!' Natalie's voice shook on a laughing protest. 'Pierce, I already feel as if I'm living in a greenhouse! Mrs Newton won't be able to find any more vases.'

'Then she'll have to buy some,' was the nonchalant retort. 'Besides, I thought all women liked flowers.'

'Of course they do—but don't you think this is rather excessive?'

'Not at all.' Pierce turned on an unrepentant grin that made her heart twist in immediate response. 'I want everyone in the world to know how I feel.'

'I rather think they've got the message loud and clear—certainly at the flower shop! Did you leave them any stock at all?'

'One or two bits and pieces.'

Pierce laid the huge bouquet down on the bedside table and turned towards the tiny, lace-bedecked crib that stood by the window.

'And how is my daughter today?'

'She's fine,' Natalie assured him, that possessive 'my daughter' doing agonising things to her insides. 'Putting on weight, and generally making up for her rather dramatic early start in life.'

'Good.'

A long finger stroked the tiny head, Pierce's face a picture of such complete devotion that Natalie found herself fiercely blinking back hot tears.

'I don't suppose I could hold—'

160

'Don't you dare!'

Natalie forced herself to assume an expression of severity in order to conceal the tangle of feelings deep inside her. Pierce's obvious delight in his baby daughter was on one hand a source of such intense joy that she thought her heart might actually burst, while on the other it created in her a desperate longing to have him look at her in that loving way, to hear his voice soften on her name as it did on his child's.

'It took me ages to get her settled after lunch, so I don't want her disturbing! She'll want feeding in a little while anyway—you can hold her then.'

'OK.' Pierce acquiesced easily, with another of those boyish grins. 'In the meantime, I'll just have to talk to my wife.'

With an effort Natalie bit back the sharp retort that rose to her lips. She should be used to this by now, she told herself. After all, she had had four weeks of watching the private love affair between her husband and her daughter grow deeper with every minute, and she had always known that her pregnancy was the only reason why Pierce had married her. But somehow just lately it had all seemed so much harder to bear.

It wasn't just that her emotions had gone haywire after the birth; there was more to it than that. From the moment that she had come round from the exhausted sleep into which she had drifted after the drama of her daughter's birth, something had changed between her and Pierce and she couldn't quite figure out just what it was.

She hadn't been aware of it at first. When she had finally surfaced to find Pierce sitting by her bed, his face pale and with deep shadows under his eyes, her first thought had been for the tiny daughter she had only seen for a brief moment before a nurse had whisked her away.

'The baby—is she all right? What—?'

'She's fine,' Pierce soothed. 'Absolutely perfect. A bit small, but that's only to be expected when she was in such a rush to get here. They've put her in an incubator to be safe, but the doctor says there's nothing to worry about.'

'Are you sure?'

'Of course I'm sure, Nat. Would I lie to you about something like that?'

'No—of course not.'

Natalie sank back against her pillows, a soft sigh escaping her as her mind went back over the dramatic events of the night. In spite of its sudden onset, her labour had actually taken hours from the time of their arrival at the hospital, the baby only finally putting in an appearance in the early hours of the following morning. For most of that time she had drifted in and out of consciousness, largely unaware of where she was or who was in the room.

Apart from Pierce. She knew that he had been with her every second, holding her hand, wiping her face, soothing her with gentle words. At all the worst moments he had been there, and, finally, at the very best of all, when he had placed her daughter in her arms for the first time.

'She'll pull round, Nat. She's a fighter, like her mother.'

Pierce's words had sounded strangely flat and inflexionless, making Natalie look at him sharply. He'd looked dead on his feet, blue eyes dull with fatigue— and something else, something she couldn't put a name to.

'Had you thought of a name?'

It had been then that it hit her. He had talked of an heir, someone to continue the Donellan line, to inherit the Manor. He had said that he would like a son to have at least one of his father's names.

'Are you disappointed?' Her tone was accusing.

'Disappointed? Why the hell should I be disappointed?' In his eyes, she saw light dawn, to be swiftly replaced by fierce, flaring anger. 'Because the baby's a girl? Do you really think I'm so bloody shallow and chauvinistic as to care?'

If she had suspected it, even for a second, then his evident fury would have driven all such foolish ideas away.

'I'm sorry—I just thought—'

'Well, you thought wrong, Nat. She's mine—my daughter—and I'll love her for the rest of my life. Damn it, she'll be able to run the estate as well as anyone if she wants to.'

'Perhaps next time...' Natalie tried tentatively, only to see his face close up, blue eyes shuttered against her.

'No,' he declared, harshly adamant. 'Never again. A "next time" is not a consideration.'

Which told her exactly where she stood on the prospect of the future. Pierce might have been forced by circumstances to have her as his wife, the mother of *this* child, but that was where it ended. No more children—and so no more reason to continue with the marriage? Suddenly all trace of the joy of her daughter's birth fled from Natalie's heart, leaving her feeling lost and desolate so that she turned her face into her pillow.

'I'd like to sleep now,' she said dismissively, and held back on her feelings until, not even bothering to make any pretence at reluctance, Pierce had gone.

Only when she heard the door closing behind him did she allow her grief to break, hot, bitter tears trickling down her cheeks and onto the crisp white cotton sheets. She had thought they were getting somewhere, coming to some sort of an understanding, but now it seemed that she had only been deceiving herself. If anything, she now had even less than before because then at least she had been the woman who was carrying Pierce's child. Now, with that baby a living, breathing entity in its own right, her husband had swiftly transferred his loyalty and concern to her without even a look back.

The harshest irony of all was that the trauma of the baby's birth had brought home to her in a way that nothing else could just how much she wanted Pierce in her life, how much she needed him. How could she possibly live with the little he was prepared to offer her in the future? And yet, deep inside, she knew that there was no way she could consider the possibility of existing without him.

'Did you manage to get any sleep this afternoon?' Pierce's voice dragged her back to the present, and in spite of the unhappiness of her thoughts she found she could nod quite easily, even managing a smile.

'Yes, thanks to your mother taking Emily for a couple of hours.' This time her smile grew without any effort on her part. 'I practically had to beg to get her back. Alice really has turned into a doting grandmother.'

'Well, don't say I didn't warn you.' Pierce perched on the side of the bed, dark and devastatingly attractive in a black T-shirt and jeans. 'Are you going to make it down to dinner tonight?'

'I don't see why not—and I might even make it through the whole meal without falling asleep. If I'm really lucky, I'll be able to squeeze into something reasonably attractive.'

'I doubt if there'll be much squeezing to do.' Pierce laughed. 'You didn't put on much weight while you were pregnant, and from what I can see you're just about back to your former gorgeous self. So, tonight I suggest you wear something to go with this.'

Smilingly he held out a slim black jeweller's box. When Natalie opened it she gasped aloud in delight at the sight of the heavy gold chain and the fine heart-shaped diamond that hung from it.

'Oh, Pierce...'

She couldn't speak for fear of bursting into tears, her heart seeming to be beating high up in her throat.

'Try it on.'

His eyes were deep, dark pools, and as she hesitated lean brown hands lifted the chain from the box and eased it around her throat, the links cool against her flesh, his fingertips brushing the delicate skin at the nape of her neck, sending a frisson of reaction shivering through her.

'There.'

He smoothed it into place, the delicate heart lying just above the soft valley between her breasts, its beauty framed by the coffee-coloured lace of her nightdress. For a second he looked straight into her eyes and Natalie was sure that he must hear the heavily accelerated beat of her heart, his fingers picking up the thudding pulse just under her skin.

'Do you like it?'

'I—love it.'

The words broke embarrassingly in the middle as she fought against the longing to tell him that she didn't need diamond hearts—that what she truly wanted, what she yearned for most of all, was the flesh-and-blood reality of his living heart, to know that it beat with love for her as it did for his daughter.

'It's just—you give me so much.'

Pierce's shrug dismissed her concern. 'It's easy to give when you have plenty.'

'But I want to give you something...' It was the nearest she dared come to declaring the way she really felt about him.

'Oh, Nat, can't you see? You've given me the greatest gift that anyone could ever wish for—our daughter.'

He would never know that his words were like another arrow in her already wounded heart, because Pierce had no idea of the gift she most longed to give him—her undying love for the rest of his life. But in spite of everything she knew she couldn't give up hope completely. Perhaps now, with him in this more gentle mood, there might be a chance of a new beginning.

'Pierce—will you tell me something?'

'What is it?'

'About Phillippa...'

It was a mistake; she knew it as soon as she saw his dark scowl, the way his eyes turned to ice as he withdrew mentally, destroying the peaceful atmosphere at once.

'Do we have to talk about her now?' he demanded harshly. 'Why—?'

But at that moment Emily stirred in her crib, gurgling softly as she flung out one arm. Within seconds her eyes had opened and, realising that she was hungry, she let out an angry wail. At once Pierce was across the room, lifting her gently, murmuring soft words of love as he carried her over to Natalie.

'All right, my princess, there's nothing to fuss about. You see, Mummy's here.'

He returned to his place at the foot of the bed as Natalie unfastened the front of her nightdress and settled the small, dark head at her breast, the baby's protests subsiding to a contented murmur as she began to suck.

'God, you don't know what it does to me to see her like that—to know she's *mine*!'

Pierce's voice was low and husky, drawing Natalie's gaze to his face to see the darkness of his eyes, the possessive intonation matched by his expression.

Suddenly it was as if she had taken a couple of steps back in time, and she could hear her own voice telling Sue that Pierce would never settle down, that he would never be faithful to any woman. Now she would never know if she had been right in her predictions for him and Phillippa, but one thing she could be sure of. Pierce *had* settled for one woman at last. His daughter would never be just one of his six-week wonders—and she was *Emily's mother*. Surely that had to count for something?

Emily was fed, changed, cuddled and settled back in her crib, and Natalie was just thinking longingly of a refreshing shower before getting changed for dinner when the sound of a car racing up the drive at speed drew Pierce to the window. What he saw there made his face change dramatically, and without a word he turned on his heel and strode from the room.

'Pierce?'

Alerted and disturbed by his behaviour, Natalie sprang out of bed and ran to the window. She was just in time to catch sight of the elegant woman who slid out of the low-slung sports car, blonde hair gleaming in the early evening sunlight, and realisation sent a blow to her heart as if she had been kicked in the chest by a mule.

'Phillippa! What's *she* doing here?'

Not pausing to think, she snatched up the silky robe that matched her nightdress, pulling it on and knotting the sash around her waist as she fled, silent in bare feet, out onto the landing, just as Pierce, unable even to wait for his former fiancée to ring the bell, pulled the front door open wide.

'Pierce!' Phillippa's voice carried clearly to where Natalie stood at the top of the stairs. 'Oh, Pierce! It's wonderful to see you!'

'Phillippa.' Natalie could interpret nothing of Pierce's mood from the single word, his voice so low that she had to strain to hear it. 'Come in—we'll go into the lounge.'

'I've missed you so much! You must know that's why I've come...'

The snatch of words was all that Natalie could catch during their brief journey across the hall, then the living-room door slammed shut, leaving the two of them alone together.

For several long, taut seconds Natalie hesitated at the head of the stairs. She couldn't, she told herself. She didn't want to know. But then again she couldn't live *not* knowing. She was in the hall before she had time to think again.

The thickness of the door muffled the sound of their voices, but by moving very close to the wood she caught Phillippa's carrying tones.

'Pierce, I was so wrong to give you up! I know that now. I made a terrible mistake.'

'So did I, Phillippa—the worst mistake of my life—'

Pierce's voice was firm and strong, the certainty in it making Natalie spin away from the door, doubling up in pain. He had admitted that he regretted what had happened, declared that giving Phillippa up without a fight was the worst mistake of his life. And why? Because, in his distress, he'd gone straight to Natalie, slept with her, got her pregnant, and because of his strong sense of responsibility had felt he had a duty to marry the mother of his child, as a result of which he was no longer free to marry the woman he loved.

'Oh, Pierce!' she whispered, wrapping her arms around her body as if by doing so she could stop herself from falling to pieces inside.

'But now I want to start again,' Phillippa was saying. 'I want to try and make it up to you.'

Her voice was suddenly surprisingly clear, sharper than before, and with a dreadful sense of shock Natalie realised just why. She must have made some sort of sound, something that had given her away, because behind her the door now stood wide open, and Pierce was framed in the doorway, his face set in unreadable lines, eyes dark and withdrawn.

'I—I'm sorry,' she began hastily. 'I shouldn't—'

'Natalie...' His tone gave away even less than his face, no trace of emotion in it. 'Come in. This concerns you too. I want you to hear it.'

No! It doesn't concern me, she wanted to say. It's up to you, and you've obviously made your mind up. I don't want you to tell me to my face that you made the worst mistake of your life when you married me. I don't want to hear how much you love Phillippa. But a weak, low voiced, 'No!' was all she could manage.

'Nat...' His voice was low but firm, allowing no argument. *'Come in.'* And she knew she had no option but to obey.

On shaky legs she walked into the room, wide brown eyes going to the woman in an elegantly tailored navy suit, who stood in the curve of the wide bay window, staring at her in confusion.

'And who are you?'

The contempt in Phillippa's voice had an effect like the sting of a whip, making Natalie draw on all her inner strength and lift her head, straightening her shoulders determinedly.

'I used to be Natalie Brennan, but now I'm Natalie Donellan,' she declared with all the hauteur she could manage. 'I am Pierce's wife.'

But for how long? The thought stabbed at her, threatening to destroy her ruthlessly imposed self-control, as Phillippa looked shocked at hearing her name and echoed in tones of disbelief, 'His *wife*?'

'And the mother of my daughter.'

She certainly hadn't expected that, Natalie reflected with a touch of triumph, seeing the finely plucked eyebrows fly upwards as bright green eyes were turned on Pierce.

'Your daughter! Pierce, she trapped you—she must have done! How do you even know it's yours?'

'I *know*.' There was no mistaking the deep conviction in the words. 'Emily is mine and she means more to me than all the world.'

And as she heard Pierce speak those words something strong and vital changed at the very centre of Natalie's thoughts. She had walked into the room feeling lost and desolate, believing that the temporary idyll of her marriage to Pierce was over, and knowing with a terrible sense of despair that if, as she very much expected it was going to, it turned out to be the only way to show him how much she loved him, then if he asked her she would set him free to be with Phillippa.

But now, after one look at his face, after seeing the glow deep in his eyes, she suddenly felt filled with a new and powerful resolve. Instinctively, her hand closed over the diamond heart at her throat, curling round it, seeming to draw strength from it, as in the back of her mind she heard Pierce's voice saying of his daughter. 'She's a fighter, like her mother.'

'We're Pierce's family now.'

'Oh, are you? And what about Pierce? How does *he* feel about all this? Does he love you?'

Phillippa's mouth curled in triumph as her sharp eyes caught the flicker of pain across Natalie's face, revealing the way she had touched on a vulnerable spot.

'And do *you* love him?'

And then it was as Natalie had known deep down it would always be if she ever came face to face with the other woman in Pierce's life. There was no way she could hide her true feelings from Phillippa, even if she tried. She might just as well declare them openly, they were so clearly written on her face. And, seeing her expression, Phillippa pounced like a hunting cat.

'Because if you do you'll know he chose *me* first—he wanted to marry me before you ever came into his life with your baby trap. You caught him on the rebound, Natalie Donellan, and that means you're only second best. Even if you do have his ring on your finger, it's only there because he was forced into it—because he had no choice.'

It was strange how those words suddenly seemed to have lost the power to hurt. Perhaps it was because she had said them to herself so often that their impact had lessened, become blunted by constant repetition, or perhaps it was because she knew that she was no longer just concerned for herself. Hadn't she promised herself that she would never let her child grow up not knowing her father as she had done? She wasn't just fighting for her own happiness, but for Pierce's—and her daughter's—too, and that made all the difference.

Taking her silence for acquiescence, Phillippa pressed home her advantage. 'So if you truly love him you'll let him go—set him free to be with the woman he really wants.'

If only Pierce would say something, give some indication of the way he was thinking! But he simply stood silently to one side, a dark, intent observer of the scene before him, no hint of his thoughts showing on his inscrutable face or in the narrowed, watchful eyes. But she had to remember Emily, Natalie reminded herself, lifting her chin defiantly.

'You couldn't be more wrong,' she declared coolly and clearly. 'If I loved Pierce, the thing I'd want most would be for him to be happy—and he could never be happy with you. You say you want him now, but for how long? How long before some other more interesting proposition comes along and you're off again—dropping him without a second thought? Do you know what it did to him when you jilted him like that? Do you even care?'

'I'm here now—'

'Oh, yes, you are! You're here when it suits you, but did you even stop and think what your turning up like this might mean? You obviously haven't taken any interest in what has happened since you took off with your new romance, haven't spared a thought for how Pierce was coping! If you had, then you'd have known he was married—known about our baby. Only someone who was thinking of herself alone would want to break up a family—take Pierce away from his child!'

'I'm not surprised you want to hold onto him!' Phillippa sneered. 'After all, he's worth millions—'

'Oh, he's worth *much* more—to me, at least!'

Sensing from the other woman's blustering tone that she was very much off balance, Natalie felt her confidence grow with every word she spoke.

'He's my daughter's father, and as such he's invaluable—no one could ever take his place! I'll tell you this, though: if in the future Pierce ever met someone—someone he couldn't live without—and he really wanted to be with her, then I could never stand in his way. But *he'd* have to ask me!'

A faint movement from the man at her side drew her eyes to Pierce's face, searching for an answer, but getting none. In the face of his unchanging silence, her new-found confidence faltered fearfully.

If he asked, she had said. But what if he did—what if he asked her to set him free *now*? If he said he wanted to be with Phillippa, what, in spite of her brave words, would she do then? She might be able to fight Phillippa, tooth and nail, but she could never, ever oppose Pierce himself.

CHAPTER ELEVEN

'PIERCE.'

Phillippa too had turned her attention to the silent man.

'Pierce, *tell her*!'

But Pierce seemed determined to let them fight it out between them, remaining stubbornly silent, no hint of anything he was feeling showing in that carefully guarded expression.

'Is it the child? Is that what's holding you back?' The edge to the blonde woman's voice revealed a new and unexpected touch of insecurity where before she had been full of conviction. 'If I'd known that you wanted a baby so much I'd have given you one—you could still have had a daughter or—'

'But not this one.' Pierce spoke at last, stopping her dead.

'This one?'

Phillippa looked stunned, shaking her head in disbelief, but Natalie couldn't drag her gaze away from Pierce, seeing the change in his face, the light in his blue eyes that hadn't been there before—had been missing, in fact, since the moment he had opened the door to find her standing outside.

'What is it about this particular brat?' Phillippa demanded, apparently unaware of the betraying harshness of her tone. 'What makes her so very special?'

'Her mother.'

Just three simple syllables, but, spoken clearly and firmly as they were, allowing for no possible argument or contradiction, to Natalie they were the most wonderful words she had ever heard.

'Her mother?' Phillippa actually rocked back on her heels. 'Her *mother*! The illegitimate daughter of your family's skivvy!'

The exclamation was dark with contempt, but somehow lacked any power to hurt. Armoured by Pierce's declaration, Natalie found that the words simply bounced off her like poisoned arrows deflected by a powerful shield.

'And God knows who her father might be.'

'Do you know something?' Pierce's voice was deliberately casual, supremely indifferent. 'The truth is that I don't give a damn. If her father was Jack the Ripper or the Emperor of China, it wouldn't alter a single thing. Natalie is herself—completely unique—a very special individual. No matter who her parents were, she is her own perfect, lovable self, and that's all I care about.'

Lovable. Natalie felt as if her head was reeling, her eyes blurring so that she couldn't see Pierce's face clearly. Had he really said *lovable*?

'Anyone could be the mother of your child!'

Phillippa tried once more, but most of the fight had gone out of her voice. Hearing the unexpected hesitation, Natalie blinked hard, clearing her vision, focusing it on Pierce's face. And then, at last, she saw what the other woman had seen.

She saw how Pierce had turned right away from Phillippa and was looking straight at her, how his eyes, dark and deeply intent, were fixed on her face, and how the emotion that until now had been totally blanked out but which had been there in his words had altered his expression, totally transforming it.

'Anyone could be the mother of my child,' he agreed slowly, holding her gaze with his so that she could not look anywhere but deep into his eyes, seeing the burning sincerity, the power of feeling in them. 'Any woman I'd slept with—had sex with. But only Natalie could ever be my wife in the truest, fullest, most powerful sense of the word.'

He was ignoring Phillippa completely now, seeming unaware that she was even still in the room.

'Nat, you said that if ever I met someone I couldn't live without you wouldn't stand in my way...'

For one terrifying second the fragile hope that had flared in Natalie's heart weakened and flickered as if in the force of some powerful draught, and a cold, creeping fear slid into her mind. But then Pierce took a couple of steps forward, reaching out to take both of her hands in his, his intent gaze never faltering for a moment.

'Well, I have—I've met someone who makes everything so much brighter simply because she exists, someone without whom the world would be empty, my life pointless. So now will you keep your word? Will you help me—let me be with her for ever?'

'Help—how?'

Could he mean what she thought he did—what she hoped—prayed with all her heart that he meant? Was it possible? Did she dare to dream?

'How can I help you?'

If she had any doubts left, then Pierce's slow, gentle smile, the soft light in his eyes dispelled them for ever, and she knew that she was not the only one to recognise that look for what it was as behind her she heard the door bang violently, slamming shut in the wake of Phillippa's precipitous departure.

She knew then that she had understood correctly, that she hadn't allowed herself to be blinded by hope, by her own dreams, her own needs. Just as Phillippa had been able to read her own love for Pierce in her eyes, so now she had also been able to see how *he* felt about Natalie.

'What shall I say to this woman?' she asked softly. 'What do you want me to tell her?'

'Tell her that I love her with all my heart—that I can't live without her—that I need her—that I want her! But most of all, please, make her tell me if she feels the same way about me. And if she does tell her to let me know before the agony of uncertainty kills me. Ask her to say if she—'

'Oh, she does!' Natalie broke in on him, unable to hold back any longer, her heart soaring, joy making the words strong and confident. 'She *does*—I do! I love you so much, Pierce—I always have.'

'And I love you.'

Suddenly realisation of what she had said hit home and Pierce's head went back sharply, his eyes darkening. *'Always?'*

'Always,' Natalie agreed with a shy smile.

'But—Nat, sweetheart, we have some talking to do—we seem to have been at cross purposes for so long.'

'So it seems. But before we talk...' She still couldn't quite believe it, couldn't get her head round the fact that he had said those magical words 'I love you'. 'Will you do something for me?'

'Anything—what is it?'

But even as she opened her mouth to answer him he had read the need in her eyes, and, coming swiftly to her side, he gathered her close, capturing her lips with his and kissing her with a passionate thoroughness that had her sighing her contentment when he finally released her.

'That better?' he asked softly, laughter lighting up his eyes as she nodded dazedly, her fingers coming up to cover her mouth as if to hold the imprint of his kiss there for ever. 'It's just a little on account till we get things sorted out.'

With her hands in his, he led her to the settee, settling her comfortably before he sank down beside her, looking deep into her eyes, his gaze dark and searching.

'So tell me—when did you first know you loved me? You said always, but you can't mean—' He broke off abruptly as Natalie nodded.

'I had the most almighty crush on you all through my schooldays, right from the moment you came to my rescue when I had the accident, and from there it just developed into something stronger. I did try to tell you—but you just laughed!'

'On your eighteenth birthday?' Pierce drew in a deep breath, pushing one hand roughly through his black hair. 'I didn't know how else to handle it, sweetheart.'

'It looked like it!' Natalie's laugh was rather shaky, but more because she was beginning to understand than as a result of any remembered hurt.

'It was either that or explode—yell at you to keep out of things you didn't understand—and that would have hurt you even more. Besides, I had no idea that you really meant it. I thought it was just the wine talking.'

'Perhaps it was. I think what I felt then was still a teenage crush—nothing like the way I came to feel.'

'But you denied it.'

'Because I didn't know how you felt and I was scared stiff.'

'You hid it pretty well.'

'You weren't exactly hearts and flowers yourself!' Natalie protested. '"Marry me or else—"' She had to break off abruptly as the words were kissed from her lips.

'Oh, I know—I know,' Pierce muttered against her mouth. 'But I couldn't think of any other way to keep you. I wanted you so desperately then—knew I couldn't live without you—and your pregnancy seemed like God's gift—What is it?'

Holding him at arm's length, Natalie put her head back and studied his face, noting the slightly raised colour in his cheeks, the betraying brightness of his eyes.

'You wanted me—*then*?' she repeated unevenly. 'Knew you couldn't live without me? Why didn't you just say so?'

'And would you have listened? Damn it, Nat, you gave me no sign—no help at all! And I knew what an appalling opinion you had of me.'

'I— Oh, God—that day at the school!'

'Exactly.' Pierce nodded, his beautiful mouth twisting slightly. 'I was left in no doubt as to just how low I came in your estimation—and the problem was, it was all true. I did have quite a track record—I wasn't what you'd call a one-woman sort of man. If you'd asked me, I'd have said I was just having fun—and perhaps, in a way, I was kicking out against my parents' insistence on duty and maturity—but, looking back, I think there was more to it than that. I think perhaps I was already halfway in love with you and I didn't know it.'

'Oh, come on, Pierce!' Natalie couldn't hold back the protest. 'You can't have been—you stayed away from me for years. You—you asked Phillippa to marry you.'

'I know.' Pierce caught both her hands in his, warm fingers closing round hers, holding them gently. 'Look, let me try and explain. All those years you were forbidden territory—it seemed that every time I looked at you all I could see were signs saying "Keep Out" and "Don't Touch"! I worked so hard at not caring about it that in the end I thought I'd convinced myself. And so I went back to London and threw myself into my work. I played hard as well, and that was how I met Phillippa.'

Once more he sighed, shaking his head at his own memories.

'I told you the honest truth when I said why I wanted to marry—I neglected to add that Phillippa was never the love of my life. We got on well enough, and she seemed eminently suitable, but from the moment she said yes I started to feel inexplicably uneasy. I had no idea why; I thought I had it all worked out.

'But then Phillippa dumped me and I headed back to Ellerby to lick my wounds—and all the way there the only thing I could think of was that *you* lived in the village. I wanted to be with you—talk to you—and so I drove like a bat out of hell up to Yorkshire. But as soon as I reached Ellerby I lost all my confidence—and so I stopped and had a couple of drinks—Dutch courage.'

'You had to get drunk in order to come to me?' The lightness of Natalie's voice showed that she was teasing. It seemed unbelievable that Pierce—confident, forceful Pierce—should actually have been afraid of facing her.

'On the contrary, the first drink was to try to distract myself from the need to see you. After all that had happened between us in the past, I wasn't at all sure you'd want to see me. I was afraid you'd shut the door in my face. But I couldn't stay away, and as soon as I set foot in your house I felt so much better. Suddenly nothing else mattered—I felt as if I belonged—at peace.'

'But all I did was snipe at you.'

'Did you?' Pierce's grin was wide. 'I enjoyed that as well. I was beginning to see that I'd only asked Phillippa to marry me out of that sense of duty I'd had drummed into me, but it wasn't until you asked me my reasons for marrying, when you said that for you it had to be all or nothing, that I realised just what was wrong— what weak, meaningless reasons I had for marrying anyone. But from that point on it got more complicated.'

'Complicated?' Natalie questioned, and got a wry-faced nod in response.

'The more I saw of you, the more I liked. I wanted to stay there with you for ever—and I wanted you.'

'But you were determined to leave.' She knew the answer as soon as she spoke, and heard Pierce's voice confirming her thoughts.

'Of course I was; I knew what would happen if I stayed, and I was right—I just never realised how apocalyptic it would be. But I didn't regret it, not for a split second. Making love with you simply confirmed what I'd known all along—that you were the one woman I really wanted, and I'd just been treading water with all the others, filling in time, waiting for you to grow up. I woke up the next morning determined to tell you—'

'And found that appalling note!' Natalie's brown eyes clouded at the memory. 'Pierce, I was just trying—'

'I know what you were doing,' Pierce put in gently. 'Or, rather, I know *now*. At the time I was furious— and then scared because I knew how I felt and it seemed it was not what you wanted at all. I wanted to try and talk things out—that's why I came to the school. I wasn't looking for Ray at all. I wanted to talk to you.'

And he had heard her holding forth about his character faults, his fickle behaviour with women!

'I'm surprised you didn't just turn and walk out for good.'

'I considered it, but once I'd seen you I couldn't go without saying something—but I'll admit I was furious, though more at myself than at you. It seemed that just when at last I knew what I really wanted my own stupid behaviour in the past was going to come between us.'

'I thought I was just one of those many women—a one-night stand.'

'Never. And if I could have come back once I'd calmed down then I swear I would have done, but then that damn crisis blew up—I *did* phone every night, sweetheart!'

'I know you did.' There was no room for doubt in her mind. 'I just wasn't there, or the phone was off the hook.'

'But I came back the first moment I could. When I discovered you were pregnant I thought fate had played into my hands at last—giving me the leverage to force you to marry me.'

'But why didn't you just say—?'

'And would you have believed me? Remember, I'd heard you telling your friend I couldn't be faithful to a woman for more than a few weeks. As far as you knew, I'd gone straight from Phillippa to you without even blinking. How could I have convinced you that *you* were the woman I really loved? And you were apparently so reluctant to marry me; even after the wedding you kept insisting it was all a sham—that you were only there because of the baby.'

'Because I thought that was how you felt too...'

'So you can see why I decided to go for broke—get my ring on your finger and *then* show you how much I loved you, even if it took the rest of my life.'

'But just now you told Phillippa you'd made the worst mistake of your life—'

'Sweetheart, you didn't hear it all. What I said was that I made the worst mistake of my life in asking her to marry me when the woman I wanted most in all the world was you.'

'And I thought all you wanted was the baby.'

'Oh, Nat—never!'

Leaning forward, Pierce pressed a warm, lingering kiss on her mouth, dispelling all her fears in the same moment that he awoke the heated, aching need that uncoiled itself deep inside her.

'Emily's a bonus—a wonderful, magical, unbelievable extra—but all I ever wanted in my life was the beautiful, warm, passionate woman who is my daughter's mother—my wife—and the only woman I've ever truly loved. You do believe that, don't you?'

How could she doubt it when it burned in his eyes, was there on his lips when he kissed her, in his hands with every caress?

'Of course I believe you,' she whispered. 'After all, you've given me so much...'

'I haven't even started yet,' Pierce assured her. 'But that reminds me—'

Reaching into his pocket, he pulled out a white envelope and held it out to her.

'I meant to give you this later, just before dinner,' he said. 'I wanted to let you see it and then I was going to tell you how I really felt, but Phillippa's arrival changed all that.'

Frowning in confusion, Natalie opened the envelope and slid out the paper it contained. To her surprise, she found herself staring at a photograph, a picture of a tall, dark man in his mid-thirties, though from the look of the print itself it had been taken some years before.

'Who—?' she began, but then something about the dark eyes caught and held her attention. 'Pierce...?'

'His name's McClare,' Pierce said gently. 'Hilton McClare.'

'*Hilton!*' Natalie's head lifted in shock. 'He—is he—?'

She didn't dare to complete the question in case she was on the wrong track, but Pierce was nodding, his smile growing in response to the look on her face.

'This is your father, Nat, darling. Your real father, not some con man out for all he can get.'

'But how—?'

'After you told me about him that first night, I vowed I'd find him for you if I could. I hired a private detective and he's been working on the problem ever since.'

He'd done this for her. Understanding what it meant to her to know who her father was, he'd tried to give her something so very important.

'Who is he?'

Pierce's face sobered. 'I'm afraid he's no longer alive, love—that's why it all happened, you see—and it explains your mother's bitterness too. Hilton McClare was a rich man—someone Nora worked for before she ever came to Ellerby—but he was also a married man. He fell in love with Nora and she with him and he planned to leave his wife and set up home with your mother. She came here and he was to follow—but unfortunately he was killed in a motorway crash before he could do so.

He never even knew she was pregnant; if he had I'm sure he would have made some provision in his will.'

'And she must have believed he had simply abandoned her.'

Pierce nodded. 'I spoke to his widow. She admitted that she knew he was planning to leave her, and so, when your mother tried to find out what was happening, she sent her a letter supposedly from her husband saying he'd changed his mind. She feels very guilty about it now, and she told me she wished she'd never done it. She gave me the photograph for you.'

'I can understand,' Natalie murmured. 'I just wish Mum had known—I don't think she ever stopped loving him.'

'Like her daughter, she was an all or nothing sort of woman,' Pierce agreed. 'But at least now you can mentally put your father's name on your birth certificate— and finally feel you know where you belong.'

'Yes, I can—Oh, Pierce, you don't know what this means to me—although, to tell you the truth, I don't need it quite so much as I did. Now that I know you love me I know exactly where I belong, and that's here, with you and Emily and—'

A disturbing memory struck her and she looked up into his loving face.

'Did you mean it when you said you wouldn't consider a second child?'

'Oh, Nat...' Pierce's voice was deep and husky with emotion. 'You went through so much that night—and all I could do was watch. I kept thinking of all my mother endured, and—'

'Shh!' Natalie silenced him by laying soft fingers across his mouth, stemming the flow of words. 'You mustn't think like that. Believe me, Emily was worth it, as I'm sure your mother must have told you you were. And you did more than just watch—you were there for me, every second of that night, and in the end it was you who put our baby into my arms. You couldn't have done anything that meant more to me—except just now, when you told me that you loved me.'

'Well, telling you I love you is only the beginning,' Pierce assured her, his eyes darkening as he reached for her again. 'Believe me, I intend to spend the rest of my life showing you that, like you, for me it's all or nothing—and in you I've found all I've ever wanted.'

'And if I have you I'll want for nothing,' Natalie whispered, knowing as she surrendered to the strength of his embrace that she would never feel second best ever again, because the power of Pierce's love would always put her first in everything.

HARLEQUIN ◆ PRESENTS®

FROM HERE TO PATERNITY

Don't miss these fun-filled romances that feature
fantastic men who *eventually* make fabulous fathers.
Ready or not...

Watch for:

November 1997—
THE UNEXPECTED CHILD (#1921)
by Kate Walker

December 1997—
HIS BABY! (#1926)
by Sharon Kendrick

FROM HERE TO PATERNITY—
men who find their way to fatherhood
by fair means, by foul, or even by default!

Available wherever Harlequin books are sold.

Take 4 bestselling love stories FREE

Plus get a FREE surprise gift!

CHRISTMAS MIRACLES

really can happen, and Christmas
dreams can come true!

BETTY NEELS,
Carole Mortimer and Rebecca Winters
bring you the magic of Christmas in this wonderful
holiday collection of romantic stories intertwined
with Christmas dreams come true.

Join three of your favorite romance authors as they
celebrate the festive season in their own special style!

Available in November at your favorite retail store.

HARLEQUIN®

Free Gift Offer

With a Free Gift proof-of-purchase
from any Harlequin® book, you can receive
a beautiful cubic zirconia pendant.

This stunning marquise-shaped stone is a genuine cubic
zirconia—accented by an 18" gold tone necklace.
(Approximate retail value $19.95)

Send for yours today...
compliments of HARLEQUIN®

To receive your free gift, a cubic zirconia pendant, send us one original proof-of-purchase, photocopies not accepted, from the back of any Harlequin Romance®, Harlequin Presents®, Harlequin Temptation®, Harlequin Superromance®, Harlequin Intrigue®, Harlequin American Romance®, or Harlequin Historicals® title available at your favorite retail outlet, together with the Free Gift Certificate, plus a check or money order for $1.65 U.S./$2.15 CAN. (do not send cash) to cover postage and handling, payable to Harlequin Free Gift Offer. We will send you the specified gift. Allow 6 to 8 weeks for delivery. Offer good until December 31, 1997, or while quantities last. Offer valid in the U.S. and Canada only.

Free Gift Certificate

Name: _____

Address: _____

City: _____ State/Province: _____ Zip/Postal Code: _____

Mail this certificate, one proof-of-purchase and a check or money order for postage and handling to: HARLEQUIN FREE GIFT OFFER 1997. In the U.S.: 3010 Walden Avenue, P.O. Box 9071, Buffalo NY 14269-9057. In Canada: P.O. Box 604, Fort Erie, Ontario L2Z 5X3.

FREE GIFT OFFER   084-KEZ

ONE PROOF-OF-PURCHASE
To collect your fabulous FREE GIFT, a cubic zirconia pendant, you must include this original proof-of-purchase for each gift with the properly completed Free Gift Certificate.

084-KEZR

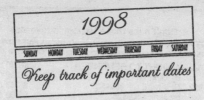

1998

SUNDAY   MONDAY   TUESDAY   WEDNESDAY   THURSDAY   FRIDAY   SATURDAY

Keep track of important dates

Three beautiful and colorful calendars that celebrate some of the most popular trends in America today.

Look for:

Just Babies—a 16 month calendar that features a full year of absolutely adorable babies!

1998 CALENDAR

Just Babies

16 months of adorable bundles of joy!

Hometown Quilts

1998 Calendar

A 16 month quilting extravaganza!

Hometown Quilts—a 16 month calendar featuring quilted art squares, plus a short history on twelve different quilt patterns.

Inspirations—a 16 month calendar with inspiring pictures and quotations.

Inspirations

A 16 month calendar that will lift your spirits and gladden your heart

Steeple Hill™

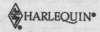 HARLEQUIN®

Value priced at $9.99 U.S./$11.99 CAN., these calendars make a perfect gift!

Available in retail outlets in August 1997.   CAL98

Don't miss these Harlequin favorites
by some of our bestselling authors! Act now and
receive a discount by ordering two or more titles!

HT#25720	A NIGHT TO REMEMBER by Gina Wilkins	$3.50 U.S. $3.99 CAN.	☐
HT#25722	CHANGE OF HEART by Janice Kaiser	$3.50 U.S. $3.99 CAN.	☐
HP#11797	A WOMAN OF PASSION by Anne Mather	$3.50 U.S. $3.99 CAN.	☐
HP#11863	ONE-MAN WOMAN by Carole Mortimer	$3.50 U.S. $3.99 CAN.	☐
HR#03356	BACHELOR'S FAMILY by Jessica Steele	$2.99 U.S. $3.50 CAN.	☐
HR#03441	RUNAWAY HONEYMOON by Ruth Jean Dale	$3.25 U.S. $3.75 CAN.	☐
HS#70715	BAREFOOT IN THE GRASS by Judith Arnold	$3.99 U.S. $4.50 CAN.	☐
HS#70729	ANOTHER MAN'S CHILD by Tara Taylor Quinn	$3.99 U.S. $4.50 CAN.	☐
HI#22361	LUCKY DEVIL by Patricia Rosemoor	$3.75 U.S. $4.25 CAN.	☐
HI#22379	PASSION IN THE FIRST DEGREE by Carla Cassidy	$3.75 U.S. $4.25 CAN.	☐
HAR#16638	LIKE FATHER, LIKE SON by Mollie Molay	$3.75 U.S. $4.25 CAN.	☐
HAR#16663	ADAM'S KISS by Mindy Neff	$3.75 U.S. $4.25 CAN.	☐
HH#28937	GABRIEL'S LADY by Ana Seymour	$4.99 U.S. $5.99 CAN.	☐
HH#28941	GIFT OF THE HEART by Miranda Jarrett	$4.99 U.S. $5.99 CAN.	☐

(limited quantities available on certain titles)

TOTAL AMOUNT	$ _____
DEDUCT: 10% DISCOUNT FOR 2+ BOOKS	$ _____
POSTAGE & HANDLING ($1.00 for one book, 50¢ for each additional)	$ _____
APPLICABLE TAXES*	$ _____
TOTAL PAYABLE	$ _____

(check or money order—please do not send cash)

To order, complete this form and send it, along with a check or money order for the total above, payable to Harlequin Books, to: **In the U.S.:** 3010 Walden Avenue, P.O. Box 9047, Buffalo, NY 14269-9047; **In Canada:** P.O. Box 613, Fort Erie, Ontario, L2A 5X3.

Name: _____

Address: _____ City: _____

State/Prov.: _____ Zip/Postal Code: _____

*New York residents remit applicable sales taxes.
Canadian residents remit applicable GST and provincial taxes.

Look us up on-line at: http://www.romance.net

HBKOD97